Summer
After
You + Me

JENNIFER SALVATO DOKTORSKI

sourcebooks
fire

Published by Sourcebooks Fire, an imprint of Sourcebooks, Inc.
P.O. Box 4410, Naperville, Illinois 60567-4410
(630) 961-3900
Fax: (630) 961-2168
www.sourcebooks.com

Library of Congress Cataloging-in-Publication data is on file with the publisher.

Printed and bound in the United States of America.
VP 10 9 8 7 6 5 4 3 2 1

To my younger and wiser sister, Melissa Collucci, who has taught kids to read, teachers to teach, and me to live.
Love you.

Chapter 1

"Spring signals the return of various species of coastal wildlife to the New Jersey shore, the place they call their summer home."

From "What's Love Got to Do with It? The Dating and Mating Habits of North American Sea Life." A junior thesis by Lucy Giordano.

I open the window shade in my third-story attic bedroom anticipating my usual—somewhat obstructed—ocean view and instead get an eyeful of Connor Malloy, sans shirt, on the roof of his parents' bungalow. Better than a mocha latte with two shots of espresso and whipped cream, as far as early-morning eye-openers and guilty pleasures go. Or at least he used to be until last fall, the Big Mistake, and the big storm— the one that tore apart our island and briefly brought together a local smart girl like me and a summer player like him. Now the guilt outweighs the pleasure.

Hammer in hand, Connor takes a nail from his mouth and taps a shingle into place. I would know those arms and that profile anywhere. I spent enough summers studying both from behind my sunglasses as Connor loped down toward the water with either a surfboard or his latest bikini-clad conquest tucked under one arm.

He stands to survey his work, glances my way, and does a double take before I can duck out of sight. My heart freezes midbeat, and I forget to breathe.

Shit. I don't want him to think I was staring, and yet I so obviously was. I should move. Why don't I move? It's like touching a scorching-hot stove top and experiencing a delay before feeling the burn. *Step away from the window, Luce. Step away.* I'm wearing a worn-out Conserve NJ Wildlife tee and tie-dye shorts, and my dirty blond hair desperately needs some sun-kissed highlights. Do I really want this to be the first time he sees me in seven months?

Connor waves his hammer at me. Too late.

"Lucy Goosey! What up?" Relief bordering on giddiness sweeps over me when he shouts his usual greeting, and I release the breath I've been holding since October. "Long time, no see."

Yes, it has been, I want to yell back, *especially if you haven't been breathing!* Maybe things are back to normal between us. I spent all winter wondering if they could or even should be. Stupidly, I thought what we shared that morning before the storm meant something. I've dissected and relived each second we were together so many times that it's like there's a permanent PowerPoint slide-show in my brain. I'd almost figured out how to shut it off. Did he even give me or what happened a second thought? Were three post-storm text messages all he needed to move on? It's not like we normally communicate during the winter months, but this year I thought…no, I *expected* him to call. Because he said he would. And like the naive genius that I am, I believed him.

I should just wave to Connor and get ready for work. I've waited too long for his attention, and right now he doesn't deserve mine. But somehow, I can't stop myself. I open the screen and poke my head out.

"Hey."

"Hey," he says with a heaviness that makes my mouth go dry.

"When'd you get down?" I ask.

It doesn't matter what direction you're coming from; in New Jersey, people who aren't from the coastal regions go "down the shore."

He shades his eyes with one hand. "Late last night. I'm helping my dad finish some repairs."

Repairs, cleanup, rebuilding: they've all become part of the lexicon around here. "Here" being the barrier islands off the coast of New Jersey. "How long are you here for?"

"Just for the three-day weekend," he says. "Wish it were longer. I wanted to blow off school on Tuesday, but I've got a game."

"It's almost summer. Then you won't have to leave," I say, although I'm not sure why I'm trying to make him feel better.

"Can't wait."

Connor and I have known each other since we were kids and have had a good thing going. For years, I relished my role as confidante to the hot boy next door—my part-time summer friend who arrived on Memorial Day weekend and left by Labor Day. And then I broke one of the most important rules we have at Breakwater Burrito, where I've worked for the past three summers. "Feed the Bennies. Don't date them." *Benny* is the locals' word for tourist, and there's sort of an unspoken pact among us to keep them at bay.

Even though summer residents like Connor aren't exactly full-fledged Bennies, I never told anyone what went down between us. My friends, Meghan and Kiki, pretty much despise all forms of summer visitors, and my brother, Liam, would *freak*. Every May when the Malloys open their house for the summer, my twin bro nods his head in the direction of their two-bedroom bungalow and mutters his perennial warning. "Stay away from that douche bag."

I appreciated that Liam thought I even had a chance with a guy like that. Look at him. With eyes the color of the clear, blue sky and wavy ash-blond hair that's always in perfect disarray, he belongs in an Abercrombie ad.

"You're so lucky you live here," Connor says.

A bitter laugh escapes my mouth. "Yeah. Lucky. We just got back ourselves. You know, since the storm turned our first floor into an indoor swimming pool."

The Malloys' house was spared any serious damage, so it's been a while since Connor or his parents have visited Seaside.

Connor backpedals. "I'm sorry... I didn't—"

I wave him off, but I'm annoyed. "No worries. Well...I'll let you get back to your roof. I've got a thing before work."

No need to bore him *or* our other neighbors with my volunteer duties harvesting baby clams for Reclam Our Waters.

"Later?" His question is so loaded with expectation that it melts my anger and resolve and tempts me to remember.

God. Must he smile at me like that? I can't say, "Put a shirt on, Connor, so I can think straight," so I search my brain for something easy. Casual. Something I would have said before the storm. Back when he was the charismatic kid who showed up every summer and I was the unabashed nerd-girl who never left—the one who knew better than to cross the line with a guy like that.

"Come by for lunch. If you order the Tsunami, I'll hook you up with a free drink." *Ugh. Lame.* The Tsunami is a mega-sized burrito that's nearly impossible for one person to eat. We ring a bell whenever someone orders it. I should have dug deeper to find the funny.

He laughs anyway. "You got it."

I duck back inside, close the screen, and pull down the shade, still hyperaware that Connor is on the other side and torn between wanting to see him again and establishing a safe distance between us. Thankfully, my baby clams and work call. I refuse to relive my brief but intense connection with Connor and accept that my love life is just one more thing that took a mega-sized hit from Superstorm Sandy.

Chapter 2

"The stretch. The male great white egret uses this attention-grabbing move during mating season. Though it sounds like an attempt to put his wing around some lovely egret lady, it's not. The male egret stands by his nest, colorful nuptial plumage bristling, leans his head back, and lets out a *cuk, cuk, cuk*! A show-offy display that makes the ladies swoon."

From "What's Love Got to Do with It? The Dating and Mating Habits of North American Sea Life." A junior thesis by Lucy Giordano.

Twenty minutes later, I'm dressed in my new *Restore the Shore* Breakwater Burrito T-shirt, jean shorts, and black Converse and weaving my hair into a long side braid. The rhythmic hammering outside my window threatens to break the mental seal around my Connor memories. I need to get out of here. I give my pale lashes two quick swipes of mascara. I hate wearing makeup, but my brown eyes look naked without it. After one last glance at the closed window shade, I tuck a peachy-pink lip gloss into my pocket before going downstairs.

Outside my bedroom door, I step lightly on the spiral

staircase. No way do I want to disturb the delicate circadian rhythms of my nocturnal brother. Liam came into this world three minutes before I did, and that was the last time he was up before me. I'm a morning person. Always have been. Liam stays up half the night listening to tunes and playing guitar, then subjects everyone to his morning moodiness. I bristle at the thought of waking him before eleven on a Saturday.

As I cross the second-floor landing to the main stairs, the scent of fresh paint and sawdust wafts up from the first floor. I hate it. I miss the way our house used to smell, like ocean mist and sunscreen. The second-floor bedrooms and mine on the third were untouched by the storm, but the downstairs had to be completely gutted. The kitchen, living room, and enclosed back porch are all new. I'm not a fan of "new." It reminds me of what we lost—and still may lose, if we don't get our rental cottage repaired.

At least we're finally home. I love Gram, but a seven-month stint at her town house in the Leisure Village retirement community is something that should never, *ever* be repeated. And yet the scary part is, without that extra rental money, it's a distinct possibility. I'm happy to be back, but the problem is, I don't know for how long.

· • ● • ·

At the marina, I lock my bike, Misty, in the rack. It took me a long time to save up 397,210 points at Lucky Leo's Arcade to earn my beach cruiser. She came with us when we evacuated, and I don't want anything happening to her now.

My ride here was unusually quiet for Memorial Day weekend with only the *whack, whack, whack* of hammers and the buzz of power saws to break the stillness. Those sounds have become as ubiquitous as the seagulls. As I walk along the dock, I'm surprised to see a big commotion at the far end of the green, under the giant 9/11 Memorial Clock. A crowd is gathering, and several news vans are parked by the curb.

I've learned to loathe cameras. We endured three years of film crews invading the town adjacent to ours as they followed so-called reality stars as they stumbled from the bars to the boardwalk and generally misrepresented the entire New Jersey coastline. Then the storm hit and the cameras returned, broadcasting to millions our personal losses and sad stories. Enough already.

I undo the combination lock on the upweller, the giant white box where the baby clams live until they're about as big as M&M's and ready to be transferred to the bay by Reclam Our Waters volunteers. I'm about to get to work cleaning containers for a new shipment of seed clams when an entourage of official-looking black SUVs pulls up behind the news vans. My curiosity gets the best of me. I check my phone. I've got some time.

I walk across the green to the clock, where I see one of Dad's friends standing on the sidewalk. "Hey, Mr. McCauley. What's going on?"

"Governor's here for another post-Sandy pep talk."

"I hope he's going to announce a new theme song. I know this sounds bad, but I'm getting kinda sick of 'Stronger Than the Storm.'"

Mr. McCauley gives me a conspiratorial grin. "You're not the only one. Maybe the gov's new best friend Bruce will loan us an outtake from 'Darkness on the Edge of Town.'"

"Ha! Maybe."

The crowd continues to grow. Two police officers move everyone away from the sidewalk. I'm eyeing the SUVs with their blacked-out windows, waiting for the governor to emerge, when a microphone pops in front of my face.

"Brenda Wills, News Twelve New Jersey. Are you a resident of Seaside Park?"

"Uh, yes. Is that camera on?"

"Not yet. Do you mind if I ask you a few questions?"

"Well, I... What kind of questions?"

"Sandy-related stuff. You know, where do you live? Did your home suffer much damage? Were you forced to relocate? What did you lose?" She rattles off her questions in an off-putting tone; one that says: *Snore, I've asked these so many times I almost can't be bothered.* I'm about to tell her *I* can't be bothered, but she plows ahead.

"Whataya say? Ready to go live?" asks Miss I-Can't-Seem-To-Mind-My-Own-Freakin'-Business. "Do you remember what you were doing on that last normal day before the storm?"

Connor's strong hands on my hips, steadying me after I tripped on the steps to the widow's walk. My heart pounding louder than the ocean. His fingertips against the small of my back. That look when he brushed the hair from my face...

I shake my head, willing away both Brenda and that day, which was anything but normal. I can't go back to that rooftop. Not now. I need to get away, and my attempt to gently push Brenda's mic out of my face turns into a swat.

"Sorry, I've got to get to work." It's not like me to be rude, and I'm super self-conscious as I head across the open lawn toward the marina, as if unbeknownst to me I'm dragging an extra-long piece of toilet paper on my shoe and people are laughing behind my back.

At the upweller, I flip open the lid. I inhale through my nose and exhale slowly through my mouth. The briny scent calms me, and visions of Connor abate. As I reach in to pull out one of the buckets, I feel a hand between my shoulder blades. I whip around.

The tension goes out of me when I see the smiling boy standing before me, wearing the same green hoodie he's owned since seventh grade. "Andrew Clark." I practically yell his full name. My boyfriend.

Chapter 3

"Clams don't fall in love. There are no courtships, fancy dinners, grand proposals, or family planning sessions. For them, it's all about the weather. When the water temperature rises above sixty-eight degrees, clams release gametes into the water, leaving a union and the creation of baby clams to chance. It's broadcast spawning. No attachments."

From "What's Love Got to Do with It? The Dating and Mating Habits of North American Sea Life." A junior thesis by Lucy Giordano.

I'm *so* not a cheater. So why do I feel like one right now? Because, like jolly old St. Nick, Connor was up on the rooftop this morning spreading his own brand of cheer and I don't know what else. Buyer's remorse maybe? And then I had my run-in with Ms. Brenda Budinski, so now I'm all messed up. I envy these baby bivalves, protected from infancy to maturity in a cozy box. They reproduce without ever touching another clam. Sex without the messy interactions or emotions. After the Big Mistake, I vowed to approach dating like an aquatic creature. Now, when it comes to love, I am a clam.

Andrew bends down to give me a quick peck on the lips, and

I feel my cheeks go red. I'm still adjusting to his recent shift from best friend to boyfriend. With thirteen years of friendship on the line, Andrew and I are still treading lightly in the romance department.

"Sorry I startled you," he says. "I called your name. I thought you heard me."

"No worries. It was all me. I was totally zoning." Assuming "obsessing over Connor Malloy" is synonymous with "zoning."

"Baby clams *can* be hypnotic."

His deadpan delivery makes me giggle. It always has. This only encourages him.

"In fact, I'll bet they're doing it on purpose."

"Doing what on purpose?"

"Hypnotizing people. It's mind control."

I bump my shoulder against his side. "Why would clams be practicing mind control?"

"To take over the world, of course."

"You read too many comic books. Clams can't take over the world. They don't have feet."

"Don't let science and reason blind you to their covert plot for world domination."

He opens his arms, and I ease into the perfect hug, breathing in the familiarity of him. His clothes smell like a combination of fabric softener and his house. Not that it's a bad thing. It's comforting. Comforting is good. Right?

"I can hold my own against evil shellfish," I mumble into his chest.

"My superhero in disguise."

"Saving the world one mollusk at a time." Someday, I hope to be a marine zoologist and work with sea mammals, but for now, Reclam Our Waters will have to do.

"What's going on over there?" he asks. We're still hugging, but I sense Andrew looking at the hoopla behind me.

I pull back and take the opportunity to scowl in Brenda's direction. "Stupid local news. Gubernatorial rah-rah stuff."

"Ah," says Andrew, showing no further interest in the governor or the crowd. He peeks into the upweller. "Want some help?"

"Sure. Can you take those buckets out? I want to rinse them with the hose."

Andrew removes the empty clam containers, and I turn on the spigot. Year-old oysters are in two of the containers. They're almost big enough to bring to a reef in the bay.

"How'd you know I was here?" I ask.

"Your dad. He said you left a note." He shakes his head. "Don't expect to see that flat screen up on the wall anytime soon. He seemed baffled by the mounting instructions."

We're still getting settled at our house and my brainy dad's not very handy. He teaches AP biology at my high school OTB—over the bridge. Same place where Mom teaches phys ed and coaches girls' basketball.

"Tell me about it. Why didn't you help him?"

Andrew flashes his *give me a break* face. "Your mom will rescue him when she gets home from work."

Andrew knows that Mom, a lifeguard captain in the summer, wears the tool belt in our family. She's been guarding beaches for twenty-some years, and she has the rep of being one tough boss. It's why my friends and I never became lifeguards.

"You're right," I say.

"She probably hid the power drill from him."

Andrew knows my family so well. He knows *me* so well. I don't remember a time when Andrew—who has always been "Andrew," never "Andy" or "Drew"—wasn't around. He's part of my posse of friends who met in preschool and grew up together playing capture the flag, crabbing on the bay, building bonfires on the beach in the off-season, and insulating ourselves from the Bennies in the summer. Andrew taught me to long board. I got him through pre-algebra.

This year, we're AP chemistry lab partners. And despite being together all the time, we weren't *together* together when the thing with Connor happened. Andrew knows everything about me, *except* what happened with Connor. I wish I could have told him. I almost did. Now the not telling feels like a lie, one that I'm afraid will come between us if he ever finds out.

"You're spacing again," Andrew says, wiggling his fingers like tentacles. "I warned you, evil mind-controllers."

I snap out of it and begin rinsing the containers that Andrew has set out in a line. "Like I said, no feet."

After years of telling people, "We're just friends," Andrew finally asked me out in January. Five months before the junior prom, and eighty-one days after the Big Mistake. I wasn't counting. Honest. The local news did it for me.

Every morning at Gram's, my parents watched the ancient TV in the kitchen, mostly to get the weather. As I sat with them eating my cereal, I'd hear: *"Good morning. It's the (insert number here) day of recovery from Superstorm Sandy. Here are some of the stories we're following for you today."* Of course all I heard was, *"Good morning. It's been thirty-seven days and Connor still hasn't called."*

We're up to Recovery Day two hundred and something by now. I lost track after I stopped waiting for Connor, started dating Andrew, and decided to eat my breakfast in front of Gram's *other* ancient TV in the living room.

Anyway, I put that all behind me, and since then, things between us have been good. Really good. Natural. Andrew and I were always close. Now we're closer. He's the nicest guy I've ever known, and I would never, ever cheat on him. Or anyone else for that matter. True, this is my first real relationship, but going forward, that's still my plan. But who knows? Forget the hypnotic power of clams. I'm bound to see Connor without a shirt again. Then what? I am the clam, that's what. That's what I need to keep telling myself. I am the clam.

"Let's put these back," I say, pointing to the rinsed containers.

The inside of the upweller looks a bit like a giant egg crate. The clams are in two rows of buckets, into which water from the bay gets pumped in and up—thus the name. While we work, applause and cheers erupt from the other side of the field.

"Sounds like the press conference is getting under way," Andrew says. "God, I hope he's here to announce we're getting a new theme song."

"That's what *I* said."

Andrew raises an eyebrow. "Perhaps one day we shall be able to communicate telepathically."

"Ew. I don't want to know what you're thinking all the time." I laugh, but what I really mean is I don't want Andrew to know what *I'm* thinking. I'm already plagued with guilt whenever Connor enters my thoughts, and he does sometimes at the worst moments. It would crush Andrew to know how I felt that day. The rush I got when I thought it was the beginning of something real and the heartache I felt when I realized that to Connor, it wasn't anything at all. It would also hurt Andrew to know that I don't want to feel that much for anyone, not again, not ever.

"I think we're done," Andrew says.

I panic for a split second, imagining he really can hear my thoughts, but recover quickly. I wipe my wet hands on the back of my shorts.

"Help me close the lid?"

"Sure thing," Andrew says.

After I lock the upweller, we walk toward my bike. Andrew's skateboard leans next to it on the rack.

I wrinkle my nose at the crowd, which has grown larger. "I'm taking Bayview to work. Where're you headed?"

"Boardwalk. Gonna fill out some job applications."

The bike rental place where Andrew used to work still hasn't reopened.

"I told you. You should apply at Breakwater Burrito. We can work together."

"Nah. I like eating there too much."

"You'd get free food."

Andrew shakes his head. "It would ruin the magic."

He worries a lot about ruining the magic. Like the time all the lights came on in the SpongeBob Fun House and we saw that what seemed so cool in the dark was nothing more than a lame, kiddie roller coaster. To this day if anyone brings it up, he's still outraged. So when he talks about ruining the magic, I know not to push it.

"Thanks for helping with the clams." I put my arms around his neck and give him a hug.

He laughs. "Just looking out for my investment."

He means the clams, not me. Andrew and his dad are big time into fishing, crabbing, and clamming. They're always teasing me about how they reap what I sow.

"Very funny," I say.

Andrew kisses me on the top of my head.

"Text you later," he says as he flips his board into position and pushes off toward the boardwalk.

"Like you!" I call after him.

Andrew gives me a backward wave without turning around. "Like you more!"

We both agreed that right now, "like" is the only *L* word we can handle. As I watch him go, all thoughts of Connor vanish—almost. I guess technically thinking about *not* thinking about Connor still counts as thinking about him, right? But it's not cheating. I swear. I'm with Andrew now, and everyone who knows us knows we're perfect for each other.

Chapter 4

"Female redhead ducks are the aggressors in duck relationships. A female will jerk her head up and down and
stand erect to catch the male's attention, and she is
not above playful nipping or dashing in front of him and
cutting off his path while swimming. Her flirtations are
deemed successful when the male returns her affections
by twirling around and showing her his backside."

*From "What's Love Got to Do with It? The Dating and Mating Habits
of North American Sea Life." A junior thesis by Lucy Giordano.*

I walk through Breakwater Burrito's back door at ten to the
sound of Bob Marley's "One Love" and the smell of pine-
apple, onions, and peppers. *Ah.* It's like I never left. The island-
themed playlist has been cued and the chopping has begun. But
underneath the familiar sounds and smells is that scent I loathe.
New. Like so many of us, Adela and Mack, Breakwater Burrito's
owners, lost a lot. They had to replace the entire kitchen, all
the floors, and every inch of Sheetrock after the storm, and it
meant using some of their own money to do it. Turns out flood
insurance doesn't cover everything.

"Lucia!" Mack says. He and Adela like to use my proper name. "Ready for the register this year?"

At thirteen, I started out busing tables, then worked as a food runner when I was fourteen and fifteen. This will be my first summer up front taking orders and money.

"Definitely," I say, though really, I'm kind of nervous. From the time we open at eleven until the time we close, the line is consistently out the door. It's awesome that so many people love our food, but it definitely adds to the pressure. I think the fact that we're only open Memorial Day weekend through Labor Day really creates a pent-up demand for "Fish Tacos, Fresh Fixings, Friendly Faces." That, and the restaurant's understated cool vibe.

"Put your stuff down, hon," Adela says. "We'll get started in a few minutes."

"Okay," I say. "Gonna wash my hands too."

I assume Adela is running our annual staff meeting this morning like she does every year. Mack, who's already up to his elbows in peeled avocados, is a trained chef and part-time musician. Food and tunes are his domains. He's the creative force of the duo. Adela? She's the boss. Staffing, scheduling, advertising, deliveries, merch (we sell shirts, hats, and necklaces), and just about everything else is handled by the ever-capable, always-smiling Adela. Have I mentioned how much I love it here?

As I exit the restroom, the door bangs open and in comes Scott, one of the line cooks who's a grade ahead of me in school. His younger brother, Jason, is starting as a bus boy this year and follows on Scott's heels. Five minutes later two more early shifters show up. Michael and Tammy are both lifelong Seaside residents. They're in college now but come home every summer to work here.

Kiki is scheduled for this morning too, but I know she'll be late. Kiki is *always* late. It's one of the reasons she drives to school with me and my parents most mornings. She's never on time for the hour-long bus ride to school. It's a good thing she works here and not with Meghan at the rescue squad. Even with lives depending on her, Kiki couldn't move any faster.

"Gather 'round, people," Adela says. "Let's get started."

Adela goes over instructions for employee hygiene, the safe and proper handling of food, and customer service. Kiki slinks in and stands beside me, winking and giving my shoulder a nudge. Her bangs are blue today. Some days they're purple. Others it's cotton-candy pink. Kiki has mood hair.

"Nice of you to join us, Karina," Adela jokes. "I hear our famous fixings bar calling your name."

"Not the salsa slog," Kiki moans.

"Early bird works the register," I say, and Michael offers a fist pump in solidarity.

After wrapping up with a quick overview of all the improvements—I can tell Adela doesn't want to dwell on the repairs—it's go time. Adela gives me a quick tutorial on the register, but after three years of observing, I'm pretty sure I know what to do. Take the order, read it back, ask if it's for here or to go, and collect payment. If they're staying, I give the customers a chrome-plated rod with a number on top to place on their table so the runners know where to deliver the food. Michael is working the register next to mine, which is for phone orders and pickup only.

"Let's do this," he yells right before Adela unlocks the door and people start streaming in. Michael's being overly dramatic, but still, I get a rush.

By noon, we're packed. Every table is filled and the line spills out the door. It's chilly for late May, but between the cuisine and the body heat, it feels like Costa Rica inside Breakwater Burrito. I'm holding my own on the register, but Michael jumps in periodically if the phones are slow to keep the line moving. The crowds are bigger than usual. Maybe it's because people are curious to see the restaurant after the storm. Not too much has changed. The most noticeable difference is the walls, which have been painted deep blue, like the sky at sundown right before it turns black. The old walls were covered with Breakwater Burrito bumper stickers, which we handed out for free and let patrons stick wherever they wanted. I honestly don't remember what color they were. I have to ask Adela if we're handing out bumper stickers this year.

At a quarter to one I start thinking about what I want to eat at break. *Taco salad or veggie taco?* That's what's going through my head as I collect the signed credit card receipt from a muscled dude so big he's casting a shadow over me, the counter, and the register. He ordered three beef tacos and a burrito, but he could've easily handled the Tsunami.

"Here you go," I say, handing him his number. "Place this on your table and someone will bring your order shortly."

When he steps aside, I stifle a gasp. Connor is standing there.

Wearing a shirt. And he's with a girl! Okay, maybe he's just standing near a girl. I can't tell. But then she cups her hand over her mouth and whispers something in his ear, and I know they are *together* together. This shouldn't be a surprise, right? Connor's always with a girl. So why do I feel like someone just stuck a plastic knife in my gut?

Pull it together, Luce. Take the high road, says the voice in my head. But that voice is muffled, like it's drowning in a sea of guacamole, and I can't help frowning as I give the whisperer a quick once-over. Strawberry blond, bikini top (In this weather? Really?), belly-button ring (Oh, that's why.), and cutoff shorts with tights underneath. (What? It's not throwback Thursday.) She's not from around here, I can tell, and though we've never met, I'm sure I hate her.

"Hey," I say. Doing my best to sound devoid of all emotion.

"Hey," Connor says. He's not giving me the teeth-to-spare smile he did earlier on the roof when he wasn't wearing a shirt. His eyes say something though, but I'm not sure what. I squint at him for a moment, puzzled by his expression. Then my good-service instincts kick in.

"Can I interest you in a Tsunami?"

Connor pats his trampoline-tight abs. "Not today. I'm watching my girlish figure."

"You can share it with your friend," I suggest, hoping the word "friend" isn't tinged with sarcasm.

Connor puts his arm around her shoulder and says, "I'm watching her girlish figure too."

Really, Connor? You need a burrito to go with all that cheese. When did he become the douche bag my brother warned me about? I want to scream, but I keep it all smiles.

"In that case, what can I get you?" And then, because I can't help myself, I tack on, "Why did you bother coming in here?"

Connor eyes stay fixed on the menu board. "Thought there was something here I wanted. I'm beginning to think I was wrong." He slides his hand from Red's shoulder to her waist, and I drop my pen on the floor, an excuse to bend down and recover. When I do, the forgotten lip gloss spills out of my pocket. I tuck it away, wipe the corners of my eyes, and stand up determined.

Connor gets two fish tacos and an iced tea. Strawberry Shortcake wants a smoothie. As I hand Connor his pole with the number eighteen, it takes all my strength not to drive it through his heart and watch him turn to dust. My fake smile vanishes as they walk away, and I guess I'm being more obvious about shooting them dirty looks than I thought, because Kiki—who's en route to the salsa bar with a tray full of toppings—catches my eye and mouths, "What's wrong?"

I shake my head and get back to work, relieved that I don't have to bring Connor and his date their food. Two customers later, Adela tells me to go on break. I was looking forward to eating here, but that plan has been trashed by the arrival of my illustrious neighbor and Belly Ring. I'm about to duck into the back and grab my things when Andrew walks in.

Yes! I could kiss him. I will kiss him. I do kiss him, right in the middle of Breakwater Burrito, two feet away from Connor's table. I can tell my PDA surprises Andrew, since neither of us likes public mushy-gushy stuff.

He clears his throat and says softly, "Well, hey. That was a warm welcome. I came for lunch."

"Perfect timing." I walk him toward the counter. "What do you want?"

I give Michael our order—taco salad for me, a beef-and-cheese burrito for Andrew, chips and guac to share—and sit down by the window in full view of Connor.

"How's the job hunt?"

"Okay. I filled out applications at the Castle Arcade, Lucky Leo's, and Donovan's Surf Shop. Then I stopped home to get my car so I could hit a few places OTB."

Two bridges—one outgoing, one incoming—span Barnegat Bay, connecting our barrier island to the rest of New Jersey. We refer to everything on the other side as OTB.

"Oh yeah? Like where?"

"Dave's WaveRunner Rental at the foot of the bridge, Stewart's Burgers… And hey, you know where I else applied?"

I smile big as I listen to Andrew while sneaking glances at Connor. Our eyes finally meet and my stomach twists. I'm the first to turn away.

"Everything okay?" Andrew turns to see where I'm looking. Covert ops are clearly not my forte.

"Just wondering where our food is." I crane my head toward the kitchen in an exaggerated motion.

"Anyway, Rafferty's looks like it's a possibility."

"Wait, what? Rafferty's? The dive bar where Liam's band plays?"

"It's not a dive. It's *rock and roll*!" He does the heavy metal head-banging thing, complete with the devil's horns hand motion, and I slink lower in my seat. "So yeah, Rafferty's. That's what I was telling you while you were stalking our food."

I take Andrew's hands in mine and focus hard on his face. "Sorry I was distracted. Just hungry."

"I see that."

"So what would you do at Rafferty's?"

"Bar back mostly. Some table busing and cleanup. Maybe they'll eventually let me help out with sound. I told the owner I have some experience."

"With sound? Since when?"

"Seventh grade. When I joined drama club for a year." His eyes bulge with incredulity.

"Because you had a crush on Rachel Thomas? Tell me, exactly when during that subpar production of *Grease* did you garner sound skills? As I recall, you spent most of your time wiping drool off your chin."

Andrew's laughing because he knows he can't fool me. "Don't you worry, baby. I know my way around a board."

"Mmm-hmm."

I'm surprised Andrew wants to work there. It's more my brother's scene. Me and Andrew, we're daytime people, and besides, I don't like the idea of us working opposite shifts.

"What made you apply there?"

"Stacie said they were looking for someone."

"Stacie who?"

"Stacie Meyers. From school. She waitresses there."

Jet-black hair? Ridiculously long eyelashes? That Stacie?

"When did she tell you this?"

"Thursday, at lunch. You went off campus with Kiki and Meghan that day. Remember?"

No. No, I don't remember. Should I? Our food arrives just as Connor gets up to leave, and thoughts of Stacie Meyers lunching with my boyfriend disappear faster than raindrops into the ocean. Connor looks back and forth between me and Andrew. Our eyes lock and he stops, leaving his date standing there holding the door. I return his glare with a tight-lipped smile, then he waves two fingers at me and walks out.

"I'm starving," I say. I jab my salad with a fork and take a bite even though I've completely lost my appetite.

Chapter 5

"Seagulls are faithful, not fickle birds. They remain attached to one mate, one colony, and one nesting ground for life. Seagull divorce is rare and not without consequences."

From "What's Love Got to Do with It? The Dating and Mating Habits of North American Sea Life." A junior thesis by Lucy Giordano.

Scuttle, the one-legged seagull, hops over as I'm spreading out my towel in the sand. I swear he recognizes me. A grin spreads across my face. It's the first time I've smiled since seeing Connor at work today.

"Got something for you," I tell him, then reach into my bag for the stale bread I brought with me. I tear off a few small pieces and throw them Scuttle's way.

"That bird's going to follow you home one day," Liam says. His wet suit's zipped and he's ready to surf. "Coming?"

"I'll catch up with you in a sec."

I was totally shocked that Liam agreed to join me. Our parents have a strict rule against surfing alone after hours without any lifeguards on duty. After work, I *so* needed to be out on the water and was disappointed that Kiki had dinner plans with her mom. I figured I'd at least *ask* my brother and was totally psyched when he said, "I'll grab our boards."

Scuttle finishes the bread I gave him, and I throw him some more. Poor guy. I always wonder how he lost his foot. Shark? Fishing line? Seagull scuffle? I hope Scuttle's injury hasn't prevented him from finding Mrs. Scuttle. I would hate to think he's all alone. He doesn't seem to hang out with the other birds, and he's definitely more skittish than the other gulls notorious for stealing chips and Cheetos right out of people's beach bags and hands.

Last summer, this group of prepubescent boys met on the beach every day for what seemed like the sole purpose of torturing him. They'd pile a bunch of snacks then throw their shoes at Scuttle as he hopped over to eat them. It was disgusting the way they amused themselves by hurting a defenseless bird. I yelled at them all the time, but they just laughed at me as I walked away. The lifeguards told them to stop too, but once their backs were turned, the boys returned to their sick game.

One day, Connor arrived at the beach and didn't hesitate when he saw what they were doing. He walked right up to the group's ringleader and told him to cut it out.

"Who's going to make me?" asked the kid, though he lacked the physique to back up his big mouth.

Connor dropped his towel and motioned toward the kid. "Let's go. Me and you, right now."

"Whatever." Mr. Big Stuff turned from Connor, backing down while his spineless friends attempted to bolster his deflated bravado, muttering things like, "He's not worth it, man."

Connor didn't let up. "Tell you what," he said, striding over to get in the kid's face and poke a finger at his scrawny chest. "I'm going to be watching you...all of you. *All* summer. Next time I see you doing that, we're going to finish this."

I saw and enjoyed the confrontation from my beach blanket, where I was lying belly-down reading my hefty Audubon guide to sea mammals. Connor picked up his towel and started walking toward me, looking for a place to sit.

"Lucy Goosey!" he called when he saw me.

"Hey, what up?" I tried to say it like he would.

"Can I sit?" he asked, pointing to my blanket.

I slid over and made room. "Sure."

He nodded toward my book. "Is that what all future marine mammalogists read on the beach?"

I liked that he got the "mammalogist" part right. "What? It's interesting."

"Really. Tell me one fascinating thing you learned in that book."

"Northern right whales have the largest testes in the animal kingdom."

"I'm surprised."

"Why? Because you thought it was you?"

Connor laughed. "No. Because blue whales are the largest. One would think they'd have the biggest cojones."

I propped myself up on my side and faced him. "Now I'm surprised."

Connor turned his body so that it was facing mine and grinned. "Because I know about blue whales?"

"Because you're bilingual."

He laughed again, and I loved how it sounded.

"Where are your friends?" he asked.

"Working or busy."

He looked over his sunglasses at me. "So I've got you all to myself?"

"Aren't we beyond meaningless flirting?"

He grabbed his heart in mock pain. "Ouch, Luce. But yeah, you're right. It's probably about time you admit how much you like me."

His eyes locked with mine and my body went hot. I was too slow with a pithy comeback, so I changed the subject. "Thank you," I said.

"For what?" He was genuinely confused.

"Saving my Scuttle."

"Scuttle?" Connor asked.

"The one-legged seagull?"

"Oh. I call him Lefty."

"I guess the obvious works too."

"Where'd you get Scuttle?"

"He's the seagull from *The Little Mermaid.*"

"Never saw it."

"You do know it features mermaids in seashell bikinis, right?" I joked.

"Very funny," he said but didn't laugh this time.

I put my hand on his arm and said, "Seriously, that meant a lot to me. I was just teasing about the mermaids. Don't hate me."

To my surprise, he placed his hand on my hip and let it linger there before he said, "Luce, I could never hate you."

"*Luce!*" Liam screams my name, and I snap back from that scorching July day to this unseasonably chilly one in May. Liam motions for me to get into the water. I grab my board and run toward the surf, duck diving through the first big wave and letting the frigid water wash over me. The Atlantic Ocean is brain-numbingly cold this time of year, which is exactly what I was counting on after work today. I love the cleansing clarity that happens when my head's submerged underwater. It's also perfect for hiding tears.

I break the surface, shake the salt water from my face, and paddle out to where Liam sits on his board, bobbing on the dark green waves and looking at the horizon. The sun at our backs shines a golden stripe between us, creating the illusion of warmth. But the chill in the air gives me goose bumps on the back of my neck.

"Finally," Liam says as I get close. Then he paddles away and waits for the next set of waves. I'm kind of glad Keeks couldn't come. Liam keeps the convo to a minimum. Neither of us is much for sharing. It's one of the few ways we are alike.

My brother turns and starts paddling toward the shore. I lose sight of him in the whitecaps for a few seconds before he stands up in one swift motion and slices through the surf, a picture of grace and balance on his board.

Liam's the kind of surfer others love to watch. Growing up, I honestly thought he'd go pro someday. My parents did too. He's more rocker than surfer these days. The whole music thing caught them by surprise. Mom and Dad always thought he was all about sports, but I've always known he loved playing guitar. It sucks sometimes how I got dubbed the smart twin while Liam got labeled the exceptional athlete with good looks to match. I guess I've embraced my role as understated and bookish. Most days I'm even proud of it. But Liam seems more concerned with railing against everyone's expectations than figuring out what he really wants.

I hang out belly-down on my board, skimming the water's surface with my fingertips as I rise and fall, letting the ocean carry me where it wants. I breathe in the fresh, clean smell and stare at the practically empty beach. Liam rides three more waves before he makes his way over to me.

"Don't turn poser on me, Luce."

Liam's challenge snaps me back to present. "I'll give you poser."

I look over my shoulder and watch for my wave. Seeing an opening, I paddle hard and prepare to get up on my board. Surfing is an exercise in patience, strength, and timing. I love everything about it. My stomach still flips in excitement each time I connect with a wave at just the right moment. It's like jumping onto a magic carpet as it takes flight.

I forget about Andrew, his lunch with Stacie, Connor, and Belly Ring girl. I stand, knees bent on my board, touching the curling wave behind me with my right hand and stretching my left arm out for balance as I guide my board and body along the cresting wave. Perfect balance. It's what I've been missing since I opened my window shade this morning and Connor knocked me off my center.

"Nice!" Liam calls.

I burst into a grin at his compliment and paddle back to him so we can wait for the next set together. Surfing has taught me a lot about life, and Mom has taught me and Liam everything we know about surfing. She always says, "Never think you're in complete control." Seeing Connor at work today was like getting hit with my board after taking a stupid risk on the waves. It stung, but on some level I deserved it for forgetting an important lesson.

My brother and I surf without talking until the sun sinks lower in the sky and we've both had enough. As we exit the water, what's left of the boardwalk's lights flicker against the evening sky. Keeks and I made plans for later tonight to meet Meghan at the south end of the boardwalk where the ride pier used to be.

We reach our blanket, and I towel-dry my hair before running a brush through it and twisting it into a knot at the base of my neck. I'm unzipping my wet suit when I hear my brother say, "Speaking of posers."

I look up to see Connor, with his surfboard and his girl, walking down the beach. His girlfriend wears a hoodie over her bikini top, concealing the belly-button ring, but for a second time today, Connor is shirtless and wearing only a swimsuit. No wet suit. Two of Connor's summer friends trail behind. Neither has a board.

"He's going to freeze his balls off," Liam says.

"One can only hope."

Liam crooks one eyebrow. "Thought he was your bud."

"He was. Is. Whatever. Let's go."

I pull a sweatshirt over my head, tie my towel around my waist, and pick up my board. Liam's already walking toward the boardwalk. I follow, taking a wide path and hoping to avoid Connor's entourage. It doesn't work. He sees me and Liam, puts down his board, and jogs our way. His friends stay behind. I wonder if he told them to.

"Hey, Luce. Giordano." He uses our last name to address Liam, which sort of suits my brother better than his first. It's funny. Liam got the Irish name and Italian looks. I got the opposite.

"Malloy," my brother says with a nod. "Better be careful. The lifeguards are off duty. There'll be no one here to save your frozen ass."

"Is the water that cold?"

"It's *May*." I'm unable to hide my incredulity. Tourists come back every year expecting the water to be as warm as when they left. Sometimes it doesn't get into the sixties until July.

I expected more from Connor. That seems to be the general theme of the day though.

My brother just laughs and walks away. I start to follow, but Connor reaches out for my arm, grazing my elbow. "Uh, Luce. Wanna stay? Surf some more?"

Is he out of his mind? No. That wouldn't be at all awkward. I sense Liam's eyes on me before he keeps walking.

"Thanks, but I'm done. Guess your girlfriend doesn't surf."

This catches Connor off guard. "What? Oh. No, she doesn't. She's not from around here."

"Neither are you, remember?" I say.

Connor looks hurt. "Come on, Luce. I didn't think it was like that between me and you."

I'm dizzy with anger right now. My eyes travel toward his girlfriend who is spreading a towel on the sand. "There's nothing between me and you, Connor. You made that clear." The words come out like pure venom. I walk away before he can answer. "Have fun."

Jerk. My hearts twists as my gaze pans up the coast, and I catch a glimpse of the Victorian house with its widow's walk. I look away. *I waited so long; first for him to call, then to see him again so I could at least ask him why he never did.* Now I know why. I get it. He didn't feel the way I did that day. He should have just said that. No need for him to throw his latest girl in my face to underscore that message, unless the message is that Connor Malloy is a total asshole. Tears escape the corners of my eyes, but I swipe them away with the back of my hand and walk faster to catch up with Liam.

Liam and I don't say anything during the short walk from the boardwalk to our house. In the backyard, we fall into the familiar routine of rinsing our boards and wet suits. Liam puts our boards in the shed while I hang our suits side by side on the clothesline. Liam's long suit next to my shorter one reminds me of Batman and Robin doing laundry. I'd say so if Andrew were here. He'd probably come back with something funnier. He always does, but it doesn't stop me from wanting to make him laugh.

I'm clipping my suit's shoulders with a clothespin when Liam emerges from the shed.

"How're things with Andrew?" he asks.

Our twin telepathy must be on. "Good. Great. Why?"

Liam shrugs. "No reason."

I change the subject. "Thought anymore about the junior prom? There's still time to change your mind." Kiki has had a crush on my brother for forever and would love to go with him.

"Nah. Proms are lame. Besides. There's always next year."

Poor Keeks. Girls love Liam, but ever since his first real girlfriend dumped him about a year ago, he's been focused on his band and not much else. Natalie wasn't just any girl. I swear, Liam had loved her since the second grade. He came home from school one day and told Mom that he was going to marry her. He's never said as much, but I think he still hopes they'll end up together. I've seen Nat around school, holding hands with other guys, and I know it must kill Liam. My brother seems rough around the edges, but really, he's a sensitive soul.

Liam walks up the deck steps to the screened porch.

"Thanks for hanging up my suit," he says.

"No problem. Thanks for surfing with me today."

"Sure." He opens the door then turns like he's remembered something. "Luce?"

"Yeah?"

There's a long pause before he answers. "You and Andrew. You guys are good together."

I smile. That's a lot of words for my brother. He lingers for a moment more, his own smile morphing into a more thoughtful expression, like he's about to say more. But then he steps onto the porch and disappears through the kitchen door.

Chapter 6

"Harbor seals could have their own reality show. They don't cheat, but they are serially monogamous, often hooking up with more than one mate per season. And it's an aggressive season at that! Lots of slapping, scratching, growling, and openmouthed threats——sounds like the Bennies that gave our shore a bad name."

From "What's Love Got to Do with It? The Dating and Mating Habits of North American Sea Life." A junior thesis by Lucy Giordano.

Connor. Clams. Tacos. Surfing. It all made for a long, weird day. But sitting in this photo booth with Meghan and Kiki on my lap? My toothy grin almost feels genuine as we squish our faces together in the frame and wait for the camera to take four successive shots. Every year we do one photo-booth shoot at the start of summer and one at the end. I have a collection taped around my bedroom mirror.

Kiki laughs when the photo strip prints out. "What's that face you're making in the last shot, Luce?"

"You mean the one that says my best friends are crushing my legs?" I joke.

Meghan pats her flat belly. "I should drop a few pounds before prom. It's only, like, two weeks away."

"Would you stop? You're gorgeous!" I say.

"True story," Kiki says.

We walk out of the arcade and onto the boardwalk, where the freaks have come out in full force for the holiday weekend. What most people don't understand about the Jersey shore is these idiots don't live here. We pass one group of nearly topless tourists girls, and I swear, one has a tiny dog tucked in her not-so-tiny cleavage. After she passes by, the three of us just look at each other and laugh.

"See, that's the kind of dumbass shit that gives this place a bad name," Meghan complains.

"Yeah, that reminds me. What the hell was Connor Malloy's girlfriend wearing today? Is there a Lady Gaga look-alike contest I don't know about? She doesn't seem like his type." Kiki's looking right at me, but I just shrug.

"I thought female was his type," Meghan says.

"I know, right?" I say.

"Was she a total bitch?" Kiki asks me. "You looked pissed when they ordered. Did Connor upset you?"

"What? No. I think I was thrown by the girl's tights." I try to sound casual.

"She was wearing tights?" Meghan asks. "What up with that?"

"Who cares? When the holiday's over, the Bennies and Gaga wannabes will go home and things will be back to normal for a while. Holiday weekends are the worst."

In my head, I'm really anticipating Connor's departure. Two more days and he'll be gone for a few weeks—at least until school's out. That thought, combined with the scent of fried boardwalk food and salt air, begins to right my world again. After all of those months of uncertainty, I'm craving the familiar.

"Prom weekends suck too," Meghan says.

She's right. Throughout May and June the motels in neighboring Seaside Heights are notorious for renting to large groups of post-prom beachgoers. In our town, no one rents to underage kids or groups, and you have to practically promise your firstborn as a security deposit.

"Sooo, are you planning to make our prom a night to remember with Andrew?" Kiki croons. She's smiling and twisting her hands like she's the wicked witch planning to throw Hansel into the oven. Not very romantic.

"Must you bring every conversation back to *s-e-x*?" I ask.

"Must you spell it out like a fifth-grader?" Kiki asks.

"Meghan, help me out here," I say.

"I'd like to, Luce, but you've known each other since preschool. What exactly are you waiting for?"

How can I tell them I don't want a night to remember with Andrew when I already have a day I can't forget? I can't. It would hurt us all to share the truth this late in the game.

"Are you nervous about the first time? Is that it?" Keeks says. "Because that's totally normal."

I don't want to talk about that with them. I don't want to

talk about it with anyone. Before Andrew became my boy-friend, I never had to answer questions like this. My friends always accepted that I was the girl with boyish interests, not the one interested in boys. I'm sure Meghan and Kiki talked all the time without me about sex, push-up bras, pedicures, and whatever else they read about in *Cosmo*. Having a guy for a best friend got me out of girl talk, and I didn't feel slighted or left out. More like relieved. Now, if they wanted to talk whale copulation, that would be a different story. I can talk sea mammal reproduction all day. Yep. No wonder Andrew is my first boyfriend.

"I'm not afraid about it being the first time. I'm afraid of messing up our friendship. What if we don't work? Can two people ever go back to being just friends after sharing some-thing that?" I'm not sure if I'm asking them or myself, or if I'm even still talking about Andrew at this point. I need to redirect this conversation. "How long did you make Mateo wait?"

"He's still waiting," Meghan says.

The shock must be evident on my face because Meghan starts laughing. "Seriously, Luce? We've been together since ninth grade. After a year I couldn't hold out anymore. But I can tell you, I can't imagine my first time being with anyone else."

Meghan is the experienced woman of our group. Somehow being in a long-term relationship makes her seem older, calmer, like she has her life under control and it's no big deal to talk about things that make me blush.

"So how did you know when it was right?" I ask.

Meghan shrugs. "I just did. And I'll never regret it if we don't work out, but we will because—"

"They're *soul mates*." Kiki finishes the sentence for her.

Soul mates. How could I forget? For a science-y girl who wants to be a doctor, Meghan is always talking about love in ways that don't exactly make sense to me. Words like "kismet," "destiny," and "soul mate" work their way into conversations about boys and some that aren't about boys. I don't want to doubt that people can have soul mates. The sandhill crane, wolves, and swans all mate for life, why not Meghan and Mateo? But while the singular devotion some animals have for each other fascinates me, I also find it confusing because it's not absolutely necessary for survival.

Why do humans place so much importance on finding their one true partner? Should Juliet have thought twice before plunging that dagger into her heart? Maybe there was another Romeo out there. Love shouldn't kill, and yet in so many of the great, tragic love stories, it does. That's why I prefer reading nonfiction and opted to do my junior thesis on mating and dating in the animal kingdom. Every junior needs to complete a twenty-page research paper, but the subject is up to us.

"What's the problem, Luce? You know you love him," Kiki says.

Here we go again. Why are we still talking about this? I choose my words carefully. "I do. The way I love you guys. But the other way? The 'in love' way? I don't know yet."

Kiki is losing her patience with me. I keep my emotions close, and she wears hers in her hair color. "What's to know?"

"We don't say it to each other."

"Maybe he's waiting for you to give him a sign," Meghan offers. "Guys need to feel secure too. They don't want to put themselves out there and risk getting hurt."

No. That would be a stupid move, wouldn't it? To make yourself vulnerable and show someone how intensely you feel about them without knowing in advance if those feelings will be reciprocated. A girl would have to be crazy to believe she's got nothing to lose by taking a chance like that. This night with my friends started out good, but now my inflated mood is collapsing in on itself like a black hole. I need to wrap up this heart-to-heart. My paper is calling.

"I'm gonna get going," I say. "I've got to work on my thesis."

"No way!" whines Kiki. "We haven't had twisty cones yet."

She's right. Our unofficial-start-of-summer ritual, which begins with a slice at Maruca's (the swirly sauce pattern is legendary) and includes the photo booth and Skee-Ball at Lucky Leo's, would be incomplete without stopping at Kohr's for ice cream. Well, *more* incomplete. They took down the giant Ferris wheel last month, so there will be no post-ice-cream ride, which kind of sucks. I loved that Ferris wheel. It was the same one my grandmother rode when she was a little girl. You could see for miles up and down the coast from the top. It remained standing after the hurricane, even after the FunTown Pier collapsed into the ocean, but now its colorful cars have been reduced to scrap metal.

"I'm getting mine dipped in cherry coating," Meghan says.

"I may get a sundae," Keeks says.

"I'm getting vanilla with rainbow sprinkles," I say.

"We know!" my friends say in unison.

It's true. I'm predictable. But from now on, I'd rather stick with what I know than be disappointed by some flashy new flavor.

At home after the boardwalk, Andrew texts me to see if I want to drive up to Asbury Park with him and Ryan to check out some local bands. He's sweet to always include me, but I don't want to be one of those girls who doesn't respect the sanctity of a bromance. Plus, it has been a *really* long day, and I just want to be alone in my room and get some work done. I've missed these light-purple walls—my framed photos of golden sunrises on the east wall and purple-tinged pastel sunsets on the west.

I still have the glow-in-the-dark stars on my ceiling from when I was eight and moved up here. Up until then, Liam and I shared a room. I thought I was going to have to fight him for the attic bedroom—the only one with a partial ocean view. But he claimed he didn't like the sloping ceilings or the spiral staircase. If you ask me, I think he was afraid of being an entire floor away from my parents.

I flip open my laptop and get to work on my thesis. I've been calling it: "What's Love Got to Do with It? The Dating and Mating Habits of North American Sea Life." My paper sets out to prove that love and monogamy aren't necessary for the survival and propagation of any given species. Sex without emotion works out just fine in the animal kingdom. In the human world, love hurts and sometimes kills. Look at Othello and Desdemona, Tristan and Iseult, Heathcliff and Catherine. After seeing Connor today, I'm more convinced than ever that people let you down and it's better to put my faith in science.

Around eleven I give up writing about the serial monogamy of harbor seals and the courting rituals of the piping plover and collapse on my bed with my earbuds in. I can see a sliver of night sky out my back window. There's a crescent moon and one bright planet. The shade is pulled tight over my other window, the one facing the ocean and Connor's house, and it's going to stay that way until Connor leaves on Monday. Why does my stomach twist every time I think of him?

I flip over so I'm facing the door and punch up something happy on my playlist. I refuse to cry. I get it. The mistake was mine, and I own it. Connor lied about how he felt that day. *He doesn't even like me.* We were never tragic lovers, just tragic. It's time to accept that—for real this time—and move on.

Chapter 7

"Northern moon snails are like undercover lovers. They burrow themselves in the sand during mating, preferring to keep their sexual activity 'behind closed doors.'"

From "What's Love Got to Do with It? The Dating and Mating Habits of North American Sea Life." A junior thesis by Lucy Giordano.

I awake with a start after midnight. I've fallen asleep in my clothes and missed three texts from Andrew. The first two are videos of the bands he's watching. The third says: Call u later. I wish I had slept straight through until morning because now I have restless everything syndrome.

I can hear my brother lightly strumming his guitar in the bedroom directly below mine. I recognize the tune. It's one he's been working on lately. He doesn't talk much about his song-writing, though I wish he did. I'd like to tell him how amazing his songs are, but I don't want him to think I'm eavesdropping. I walk downstairs to the kitchen and grab a bottle of water from the fridge. Everything is dark except for the light above the stove. My parents have been asleep for hours. Teachers. It's like every day is a school day. Even weekends.

As predicted, the TV still isn't hooked up in the living room, so I cut through the enclosed porch off the kitchen and step outside. I make a beeline for the bench swing that sits in the corner of the yard between our rental cottage and the Malloys' property. I lie down on its cushioned seat and dangle one leg over the side so I can rock the swing with my bare foot. Once I've got a nice rhythm going, I text Andrew back.

First, I comment on the band videos saying the same thing about both. Cool! Andrew would have said something more worthy of an iTunes review, but right now, that's all I got. I send a third reply telling him I'll call him in the morning. Knowing Andrew, he'll want to give me the play-by-play of his night. But if I stay up much later, I'll be off-kilter at work tomorrow.

I put my phone down and look at the stars, wrapping my arms around myself for warmth. The wind is blowing from the east, making the neighbor's fish-shaped windsock snap like a sail. I wish I'd worn a sweatshirt and, perhaps more importantly, socks. I'm thinking about going back inside when I hear feet crunching on the bed of white pebbles in our yard. My muscles tighten, and I push myself into the sitting position to see Connor walking my way. Like a cat, his eyes shine in the dark. My breath catches in my throat and my chills turn to goose bumps. I want it to stop; he can't keep making me feel this way.

"Hey," he says.

"Hey, yourself. Whatcha doing out here?" I ask.

"Couldn't sleep. You?"

"Just woke up."

Connor points to the swing. "Okay if I sit?" I nod.

He lowers himself onto the opposite end, as if I've got coo-ties. From a distance, we probably look absurd sitting so far apart. I'm about to say so but think better of it.

"How was surfing?" I ask.

He laughs. "Cold."

Where's his girlfriend? I wonder. Is she staying with his family? A friend? Is she really his girlfriend, and for how long?

"So," he says.

"So."

"Sorry about today."

I play dumb. "For what?"

"Not ordering the Tsunami."

"Don't be sorry. Not many people can handle it."

He shakes his head and looks down. "Having Bryn there didn't help."

"You mean because she doesn't eat solid food?"

"Something like that."

"Where is Bryn?"

He glances at his bungalow. "Sleeping." And then before I have time to wonder... "I'm on the couch this weekend."

The thought of her sleeping in Connor's bed, even if she is sleeping there alone, bothers me. *Will he sneak up there later? Just how close are they? Why do I care?* I swallow hard and nod.

Connor keeps talking. "So. You and Drew?"

Connor has met all my friends at one time or another over the years.

"Yeah, me and *Andrew*. He hates to be called Drew."

Connor half smiles. "Does he? I'll have to remember that."

"What about Bryn? What does she hate to be called?" I grin but inside I'm dying.

He chuckles and ignores my question. "So *Andrew*. Who would have thought?"

That pisses me off because, hello! Everyone I know "would have thought." I fire back, "So you and Bryn. Who would have thought? You've never had a girl stay for an entire weekend before."

"It's not like that. She invited herself. Wants to know where she'll be staying after prom."

He looks and sounds annoyed. I am too. Is Bryn more than just a passing thing? "You asked her to your prom?"

"Her prom. She asked me. We don't have a junior prom at my high school."

"So it's serious." My chest tightens as I say it out loud.

One corner of his mouth turns up. "Remember what I told you last summer? When you asked the same thing about that girl from the yacht club?"

"I remember." I muster my best Connor voice. "*Luce, my wife hasn't even been born yet.*"

We both laugh, but inside my mixed emotions are tripping and falling all over themselves. I remember the night he said that, remember everything about last summer as it pertained to Connor Malloy. While his love life remained its usual revolving door, I felt like our friendship had grown stronger. He met me out here a lot to swing and talk—about my work with the baby clams, college choices, his plans to build a permanent home here someday, kayaking. He has never done the latter and I promised I'd take him out on the bay.

I felt superior to those other girls he'd hang out with. I knew they wouldn't last until Labor Day because…I don't know, he seemed to want to be around me more often. And I found myself looking forward to being around him. Not because he was easy to look at but because he was easy to talk to. Maybe I built it up in my mind. Either that or I was stupid enough to think a boy like Connor could change. It's just that, last summer I thought he was being real with me.

We fall silent. Connor stretches his long legs in front of him and rocks the swing with his heels. I wish I could lie down and rest my head on his knee like I did that night last August. I was exhausted after working a double shift. Connor patted his thigh and said, "Here. I won't bite. Promise." When I lay down, he rested his arm on my side.

Lying there under his touch felt right, like it was where I was supposed to be. That was the night I started thinking something might happen between us before the summer ended. Nothing did. Until October. When he was here helping his parents get ready for the storm.

Since then, I've gone from never dating anyone to having a boyfriend. A boyfriend who was one of my very first friends. I knew what I was risking saying "yes" to Andrew in the first place, and there's no way I'm going screw up what we have now.

I plant both feet on the ground to stop the swing. "I should get back inside."

I stand to leave and so does Connor. He moves in front of me, blocking my direct path back to the house. "Wait…Luce? Can I ask you something?"

He takes a step toward me, and though he's still at arm's length, he's close enough for me to smell a hint of cologne. It's fresh, not perfume-y. The scent I tried to recall all winter, every time I thought of Connor. Had I known the brand, I would have bought it. It sounds incredibly melodramatic and corny, I know. But everything was so surreal after Sandy. We weren't in our home, and my friends were all spread out. Nothing felt right, including me. Not knowing what Connor felt was a huge and unwelcome distraction, and yet I still longed for some tangible reminder of our time together. I wanted something to hold on to because it was starting to feel like it never happened.

I look up at him now but find it hard to make eye contact, fearing those desperate thoughts are all over my face. "What did you want to ask me?"

"You and Drew. Are you guys serious?"

Andrew, I think. But don't say it. I shake my head slightly, and it feels like a betrayal. "We've been going out since January, but we're taking it slow."

Connor looks confused. "Wait…January? I thought—"

Now I'm confused. "What?"

Connor's jaw tightens and he shakes his head. "Nothing. I thought it was longer."

I take a step closer and force him to look at me. "Why? What made you think that?"

His face softens and he stares at me, practically through me, and I forget to breathe.

"Please tell me," I say. "Why did you think Andrew and I have been together longer?"

Still nothing. Our street is quiet tonight. No cars. No carrying voices. Only the ocean's boom.

I clench my fists and wait another second before giving up. "Forget it." I move to get around him, but he reaches for my hand. Our fingertips touch. I close my eyes, ignore the magnetic pull between us, and keep walking. That's when he places his hand on my shoulder.

"No, wait, Luce. Hold on a sec. Please? I'm sorry."

I glance toward my house, then his, half worried about being seen out here together, but willing to chance it to hear what he has to say. I nod at him to go on and he does. "I guess...I thought he was the reason you never called me back."

Whoa. Wait. What? I take a step back and his hand falls away. "Called you *back*? What are you talking about? You never called." I try not to sound bitter, but dammit, *I waited eighty-one days!*

"Yes, I did. Right after the storm. Well, not right after. I was without cell service for a few days. But as soon as I could, I called. I said I would."

"I never got a voice mail." My thoughts become frantic. Did I miss a "missed call"? Did calls not get through while my phone was dead? Communications were spotty after the hurricane, and it was difficult to keep our phones charged without power. We had to use the cars' batteries, and Dad didn't want us wasting gas.

Connor shakes his head. "I didn't leave a voice mail. Liam answered. Said you were out with your boyfriend and must have forgotten your phone. I told him I was on my way down. I wanted to see you. He was supposed to give you the message. I didn't care that there was another guy. I wanted to see you anyway."

My hands are shaking and I fear my voice might too. "My boyfriend? Liam never told me you called. Are you sure it was him? Maybe you dialed wrong." I'm grasping for a logical explanation.

"No, it was your brother. He called me 'Malloy' with the usual contempt in his voice that's hard to miss."

"Is it possible he said 'Andrew' and you just thought he meant 'boyfriend'? That makes no sense. I wasn't with Andrew then. I had just been with…"

My head starts spinning, and my heart beats out of control. I take a deep breath. I can't believe this. Why would Liam lie? He hates Connor, but what about me, his sister?

"So…wait," Connor begins. "Liam never told you I called?"

I shake my head.

"And you didn't have a boyfriend?"

"Of course not, Connor."

Connor lets out an anger-tinged laugh, and I imagine I

know what he's thinking. It's like a trainload of would'ves and could'ves just passed us by. I can almost feel the breeze, hear the swoosh. The expression on Connor's face tells me he's standing on the platform beside me, watching the train and wishing we could send it back to the station. I want him to wrap his arms around me, warm the chill that's traveling down my spine, but he can't. We're here now. At the junction of Andrew and Bryn.

"Why didn't you call me again?" I ask. "You should have asked *me* if I had a boyfriend."

Connor runs his fingers through his hair and looks up at the sky, like he's thinking or doesn't want to answer, or both. Finally, he sighs.

"Honestly? I was pissed. And hurt. I thought Liam was telling the truth. I figured you got the message and didn't want to see me because you regretted what happened between us. Still, I thought about calling you a hundred times. Then you finally sent that text, like, ten days later: SAW YOUR HOUSE. OUTSIDE LOOKS FINE. It wasn't what I expected. You sounded, I don't know, angry?"

He thought about me a hundred times? If only I'd known. I would have said more. *Why did I use all caps?* His text back was so curt. TX. That was it. No words, just two letters, a jab and hook that knocked me breathless. Without stopping to think, I fired back: I MADE A BIG MISTAKE. At first, Connor thought I was talking about his beach house, until I texted back. About us. I cried when I read his reply. Me too.

I reread his text every day for weeks. My finger hovering over the keypad as I searched my brain for the right thing to say. The words that would erase that awful exchange and make him want to talk to me. I never found them. That was my last communication with Connor until I opened the window this morning. So, here we are.

I shake my head and wrap my arms around myself. My eyes fill with tears and I can't look at him. I have to fight the urge to stomp my foot and throw a toddler-sized tantrum. "I shouldn't have said—" I whisper. "Just… I kept waiting… I didn't know you called. I thought I *had* made a mistake."

Connor closes the small space between us and puts his hands on my shoulders again. His thumbs trace my collarbone and travel up my neck toward my chin. My entire body pulses. I stare down at my bare feet and listen as my heart pounds my eardrums like a snare.

"Luce?" He bends his head, forcing me to look up at him. Our eyes meet and he leans his forehead against mine, then brushes my cheek with his lips. *I want this, I want this, I want this*, my heart sings. I tilt my head, our lips almost touch, and then… *I can't.* Closing my eyes, I lay my hands against his chest and fight back tears when I see the disappointment on his face.

"I'm so sorry, Connor, I… This isn't cool. It's not right—"

I shrug away from him, but he grabs both my hands and locks his fingers with mine, just like he did that day. I want to pick up where we left off and immediately hate myself for thinking it. I break free and run toward my house. I hear Connor's footsteps behind me as I race onto the screened porch.

"Luce, wait," he says in a loud whisper. "Don't go."

I ignore him as I step into the kitchen, panting as if I've run a mile on sand, not ten feet across the yard to my house. I wait until I'm sure he won't follow me, then I close the door behind me and click the deadbolt into place. I almost laugh at the futility of the move. I can keep Connor out, but everything I've ever felt for him and all my regrets are locked here inside with me.

Chapter 8

"Siblicide. It sounds cruel, but the survival of many bird species like osprey, owls, egrets, and kingfishers depends upon some chicks offing their brothers and sisters."

From "What's Love Got to Do with It? The Dating and Mating Habits of North American Sea Life." A junior thesis by Lucy Giordano.

I press my back against the locked door and slide down below the glass pane so Connor can't see me. My heart beats faster than hummingbird wings. I wrap my arms around my bent legs and breathe deeply. Connor called. He *called*. Just like he said he would. It's like finding out I won the lottery after tearing up the ticket. My heart aches over the conversation I never got to have.

Instead, all winter, imaginary talks with Connor buzzed in my head like white noise. And they all concluded the same way: I'd made a huge mistake. A mistake that I wanted to erase. Talking about it would have been like etching it in ink. So I decided to keep Connor a secret from my friends and vowed to stop pursuing him if he didn't feel the same way. Except, apparently, he *did*!

Ugh. I want to slap my evil twin across the face. If we were baby birds, I'd save myself and push Liam right out of the nest. At this moment, I'm not above siblicide. *Why did Liam lie to Connor? Why didn't he tell me Connor called?* I scowl at the ceiling. Suddenly, his guitar playing mocks me. It's not music anymore but the sound of his chronic indifference. *You and Andrew. You guys are good together*, he said to me this afternoon. He's so full of shit!

"You suck, Liam. You know that?" I say out loud. What he did was more than forgetfulness or indifference; it was interference.

I hear Connor's footsteps crunching on the stones outside and know he's gone back to his house. It's safe to get up, but I prefer to stay here on the tile floor—deflated. Thanks to our new open plan (we were told the updated design would increase our home's value), I can see the entire first floor from my vantage point.

The flat-screen TV lies on the table in the area formerly known as our dining room, and the freshly painted walls remain bare. The lack of hominess bothers me, but the vacant spot at the foot of the steps, where my saltwater fish tank used to be, leaves me hollow. Every time I think about my fish and the sea star Andrew gave me for Christmas, I get sick. Six months ago neither Dad nor I said a word when he unplugged the filter and heater, along with all the lights and appliances, before we evacuated. Maybe at that point, we were all still hoping for the best.

I took off on my bike on that Sunday morning, the "last normal day" as Brenda What's-Her-Face likes to call it. I was freaked out by my parents' frantic evacuation prep and had to get out of there.

"I should check on the clams," I said.

"The clams? Honey, you've got to pack. The clams will be fine." Mom didn't share Dad's and my affinity for sea life.

"Please? I won't be long. Promise. There's plenty of time to get my stuff together."

"We have to leave by *four*." Her worry started to sound like anger.

"That's in, like, eight hours," I whined. "Liam isn't even up yet." I had her there. She knew it and so did Dad. Parents aren't supposed to have favorites, and I was certain Mom loved us both the same. But Liam? Liam was her baby boy.

"Let her go," Dad said. "Be back in two hours."

I smiled big at him. Me? I was Daddy's little girl.

"I will. Thanks."

The clams were merely an excuse. Clams are pretty self-sufficient as sea creatures go, but I didn't want to lie so I jumped on my bike and made a quick pass at the upweller to make sure the lid was secure before heading to the boardwalk. The scarecrows from the annual Build-Your-Own Scarecrow contest sponsored by the garden club strained to stay up in the already powerful onshore breeze. They were an ominous sight, bolstered by wooden crosses that brought to mind Calvary more than Halloween. Along the way, I passed no one—not one person walking a dog or taking a jog—and there were hardly any cars on the road. Had everyone left already? Were they holed up waiting for the storm? Sundays were usually quiet in Seaside, but this wasn't quiet; it was still. Scary still.

On Ocean Avenue, not a single car was parked on the street. I had the urge to yell. To hear my voice echo. I rode up the nearest boardwalk ramp and turned left toward the Heights, that ten-block stretch of bars and amusements that had somehow come to define the entire coast. Along the way, I finally passed a few people who had pulled their cars next to the boardwalk to fill sandbags meant to keep the water from seeping under doors and into basement windows. But I remember thinking, given the amount of anxiety I had witnessed at my house that morning, shouldn't it look like there's an evacuation going on? Where was everybody?

When I reached the ride pier on the south end of the boardwalk, I saw a few more people taking pictures of the rising water that was already churning up pretty good. The giant Ferris wheel loomed above, its cars swaying only slightly in the wind.

I passed the arcades, Brothers Pizza, the Bon Jovi stage—where my parents constantly reminded us the video for "In and Out of Love" was shot—the second ride pier and the Jet Star roller coaster (which has since become the poster child of Sandy's destruction of the Jersey shore), and the sky ride. During the summer, the air smelled delicious: sausage and peppers, cheesesteaks, funnel cakes. That day, with the storm doors pulled down tightly across the storefronts, it smelled like fear.

At the boardwalk's end, I circled back toward Seaside Park

and home. Right before the beach patrol and lifeguard station, I switched from the boardwalk to the street. I wanted to get a better look at the oceanfront mansions, to see if people were boarding up windows and putting down sandbags. Those houses were closest to the ocean and most had been there a long time. When my brother and I were little, we used to pick out our favorite—the one we wanted to buy someday when we older and rich. (That was before he and my friends started talking about leaving here forever when they graduated.)

Back then, Liam always changed his mind about the house he liked best. But my pick was always the same: the Victorian at the corner of Ocean and Island. Over the years, it had been painted and trimmed in various pastel colors, like a dollhouse. The wrap-around porch, with its wicker swing and Adirondack chairs, was surrounded by hydrangea bushes that bloomed each summer with giant snowball-like flowers.

The best part of the house though, if you asked me, was the widow's walk. I was staring at it that day as I rode by, thinking about how I could spend hours up there dreaming, when someone called my name. Connor Malloy. On the porch of my favorite house. I hadn't seen him since he left on Labor Day.

I put up my hand to wave, intending to ride by, but Connor motioned me over.

"Got a sec?" he called. "You've got to see the inside of this place!"

I rode up the front path and parked my bike at the foot of the steps, my pulse racing as I walked toward Connor on the porch of "my house"—suddenly aware of how much I'd always wanted both.

"What are you doing here?"

"My parents are friends with the Alexanders. They keep a spare key at our house."

He held up a single key attached to an inordinately large, sparkly sea horse.

"Nice key chain."

"My mom's idea. She doesn't want to misplace it," he said.

"In case what? You need to ride over here before a hurricane and let yourself in?"

"Exactly."

"I'm serious."

"So am I," he said. "Bob and Jane are in Italy. They called my parents to ask if we'd check on the house. You know, put away the patio furniture, unplug the appliances, pull down the storm windows. My parents are busy with their own storm prep so I volunteered to come over here and batten down the hatches."

Connor was always so upbeat. He made preparing for a hurricane sound like a pig roast. He had stopped talking and was standing there with that lit-from-within smile.

"Do you know hatches were deck openings on old British sailing ships? They had to be covered with tarpaulins during rough waters and storms, and the sailors used pieces of wood, called battens or batons or something like that, to hold the tarps down…"

I trailed off because I was beginning to bore myself. When I got nervous, rattling off facts calmed me down. It also made me appear a touch crazy, but Connor seemed unfazed by my impromptu hatch lesson.

"Come on, I know you want to see it."

"Do you use that line a lot? How's it working for you?" I teased.

"Pretty well, if you must know."

I wriggled my nose in disgust and turned away as if I was leaving.

"I was joking, Luce! Come back." He motioned me up the steps with a nod of his head.

I shrugged as I walked toward him, pretending that I was in complete control and his playful tone hadn't just turned my insides to Jell-O. In truth, my mind was screaming: *You're going to be alone in that house with Connor Malloy!* And I was border-line giddy about that.

"You're sure this is okay?" I asked myself more than him.

"I told you. This house belongs to my parents' friends from the yacht club. They want me here. Got the alarm code and everything. I've already been inside."

I always wondered what kind of people, aside from the obvi-ously very rich, would own a two-million-dollar home like this and only use it three months out of the year. All shore prop-erty is expensive. Ocean views cost the most, but bay views were a close second. Even a cozy bungalow here on the barrier islands sold for double or triple what it would cost elsewhere. But these houses were in a class by themselves.

Connor opened the gorgeous double doors, each with

half-moon stained-glass windows on the top, and motioned me inside. "After you."

The house had that distinct yet hard-to-describe smell of a beach home that had been closed up for a while. I walked to the center of the high-ceilinged foyer and immediately pictured pine garland and twinkling white lights wrapped around the sweeping banister.

"Wow. I'd love to spend Christmas here," I said and immediately regretted being so sappy.

Connor smiled. "You could fit a twelve-foot tree in this hallway."

I admit, over the years I've had my share of Connor-centric fantasies. However the image of him watching his children pad down the stairs on Christmas morning had never been one of them…until that very second. I liked thinking about Connor that way.

"Come on. You've got to see the master bedroom."

The wholesome image of a Malloy family Christmas vanished. *Aha*, I thought. That was the Connor I knew.

"Uh-uh," I said. "The widow's walk. I want to go there first."

"Race you," he said and took off running.

He beat me up the two flights and was waiting for me in the third-floor hallway toward the back of the house. Off the hallway was an art studio with a drafting table and a bookcase. There was also a telescope standing near the window.

"Follow me." He crossed the studio and unlocked the dead-bolt to the narrow door leading outside.

"You've already been up there?"

"First thing I did when I got here," Connor said.

"Not the master bedroom?"

"Nah, that's the first thing I wanted to do when *you* got here."

I thought it was just more flirty banter, but Connor's flushed cheeks looked as warm as my body felt. He stared at me for a beat too long and my throat constricted. I was suddenly aware that I'd left the house with slept-on hair and no mascara. The look on Connor's face told me he hadn't noticed. His eyes never left mine.

Finally he said, "Come on, Luce. I'll follow you." The space was tight when I passed in front of him, and the closeness of his body gave me the shivers. I opened the door and stepped outside onto a small patio. I walked toward the wrought-iron spiral staircase that lead to the widow's walk on the roof and placed my hand on the railing. My knees felt shaky as I began the climb, but I never looked back.

Chapter 9

"Monogamy is an anomaly in the animal world. Seagulls and the highly selective albatross both mate for life. But for many other creatures, like the sea horse and the harbor seal, seasonal devotion (a.k.a. summer lovin') seems to be the way to go."

From "What's Love Got to Do with It? The Dating and Mating Habits of North American Sea Life." A junior thesis by Lucy Giordano.

I hear the toilet flush overhead followed by the opening and closing of two doors. *Liam.* I push myself up from the kitchen floor and rush toward the stairs, taking them two by two. I'm about to grab the doorknob and barge into his room, just to piss him off, but stop short. If I get all up in Liam's face about Connor Malloy at one in the morning, he'll know it's about more than a missed phone message. Plus, I run the risk of waking my parents. The Big Mistake has been the Big Secret for all these months. Now is not the time for the Big Reveal.

Liam, who has been playing some classic-rock guitar riff while I stand in the hallway, stops mid-strum, like his twin senses have finally kicked in and he knows I'm on the other side of the door. I hold my breath and take baby steps backward, hoping he'll resume playing and I can speed up my retreat, but instead his door swings open and I gasp.

"Shit, Liam. You scared me."

"What are you doing up?" I don't like the way he says *you*, like I've wronged him. He's wronged *me*. I didn't want to do this tonight, but now? Now, he's going to get it.

I push past him into his room. He follows, closing the door behind him.

"I couldn't sleep. Is that all right with you?"

"That's why you were in the yard with Malloy? *He's* the cure for insomnia? Ever hear of warm milk?"

"Does anyone really drink warm milk when they can't sleep, Liam? And what the hell? Were you spying on me?"

"Looking out my window isn't spying. Anyway, why are you asking? Were you doing anything to make spying worth my time?"

"We were just talking."

"About what?"

"Funny you should ask. About *you*. You know, how you lied and told Connor I was out with my boyfriend."

"What? When?"

"Uh, when we were staying at Gram's?"

"I don't remember," Liam says. I can tell from his tone that he's lying.

"Let me jump-start your memory. My phone rings. You

invade my privacy and answer it. Seven months later, I finally get the message. Sound familiar?"

I can practically see his brain spinning an excuse as I wait for his answer. "Oh, that's right. You were in the shower."

"*And what?* It seemed like a good time to answer my phone and lie to Connor about me having a boyfriend? Everything about that is wrong, Liam. If I did that, you'd go ballistic."

"What's the big deal? I saw who it was and thought maybe he had information about our house."

"That's not what Connor said."

"You're going to believe him over me?"

"Don't turn this around," I hiss. "Why didn't you give me the message?"

"Who cares? It was just Malloy. What would it matter if you had a boyfriend? Wait... Is there something going on between you two?"

I clench my fists. *I knew it.* I should have gone straight to my room. His nonchalance makes me want to punch him.

"*No,* Liam. Nothing's going on."

"Good. Because that would be cheating and you're better than that, Luce."

"I didn't have a boyfriend in November, Liam."

"You have one now."

"What the... Ugh, Liam! This isn't about me. It's about *you* not giving me a phone message."

"Don't do to Andrew what Nat did to me."

The pained look on Liam's face takes some of the heat out of my fury.

"Natalie cheated on you?" This is news to me. Liam hasn't mentioned her since the breakup. "With who?"

"Some guy in a band. That's what broke us up."

A band? Is that why he ditched surfing in favor of music? "Liam, I'm sorry. I didn't know."

I wonder if *anyone* knows. Who does my brother confide in about stuff like this? Or maybe he's like me and keeps the painful moments a secret. Liam sits down on his bed. He looks defeated. "Shit happens, right?"

"I wish it hadn't happened to you," I say.

"Yeah, well. After we were done, Nat seemed determined to hook up with every guy she met. Including Malloy."

A cartoon cannon blows a cartoon hole through my cartoon gut. Liam is studying my face as if he expects some big reaction from this revelation, but I've got my game face on. "Ha!" I scoff. "Who *hasn't* hooked up with Malloy?"

Liam looks satisfied. "Exactly, Luce. Like I said, you're too good for that prick."

"I'm with *Andrew*," I say, and that should be the end of it. Instead it's like someone lights a firecracker in my brain and my exploding thoughts rocket off in different directions.

"I haven't forgotten. Have you?" Liam asks quietly. Now I wonder how long he was spying on me and what he saw.

"I'm not the forgetful one. That would be *you*." I chuck a pillow at him as I walk out, closing the door behind me.

I hold it together until I get to my room, then I throw myself onto my bed and bury my face in my quilt. I give the mattress three quick jabs. Tears fill my eyes, but I lift my head and swipe them away. No. I can't. I want to stop feeling so much. I need normal. I pick up my phone and text Andrew. Call when u can. xo L.

I flop back on my pillow and recap the last hour while I wait. Connor called. Liam didn't tell me. Natalie cheated on Liam, and Connor hooked up with her before we were together. The thought of that last part stirs unexpected sadness and jealousy in me. And that makes me feel like shit because I have a boyfriend and none of this should matter. And P.S.: I've never been the type of girl who wanted or needed a boyfriend.

"Thank God you're not boy crazy," Mom had declared proudly more than once. Except just the thought of Connor's lips on mine, his hand at the base of my neck, does make me crazy. What's happening to me?

In seventh grade at a school across the bridge, my tight circle of friends was subsumed into a student population literally ten times the size of what I was used to at our tiny K–6 elementary school here on the island. Everyone in junior high seemed so much older than me, even though they weren't. Kiki, Meghan, and I started eating lunch with this girl Becca and two of her friends, whose names I can't really remember. It was six to a table, and we had three days to pick the kids who would become our permanent lunch buddies.

By the second week of school, I was already regretting that

Becca and company had become ours. They were *always* talking about boys. Some days Kiki and Meghan joined in. Me? I usually read a book or thought about what I would be doing after school. I looked forward to the bus ride home more than anything. I never got tired of seeing Barnegat Bay and my island town from the bridge.

So after three weeks of sitting together, right around the end of September, out of nowhere Becca asked, "So, Luce, what's the deal with you and Andrew?"

I swallowed my mouthful of ham and cheese. "The deal?"

"Yeah, like are you together? You know, boyfriend and girlfriend?"

I had just gotten accepted to a Saturday morning program for kids with a high aptitude for science, and that's all I could think about—that and the saltwater fish tank my parents were finally letting me get. Dating Andrew? Uh. Yuck. Thankfully Keeks jumped in to save me.

"Andrew is just a friend…to all of us. We grew up together," she told Becca.

"Uh-huh. Well, if you girls *are* interested, it's time to make a move. If you don't, someone else will."

Seventh-grade girls were lining up to flirt with Andrew? Would he notice a move if he saw one? I doubted it. At that point, he still collected action figures. I remember thinking I should warn him on the bus ride home. The thing is, before Becca said that about Andrew, I'd never thought about losing him to anyone. It scared me. Still does.

My phone vibrates, interrupting thoughts of our seventh-grade lunch table, but not before I remember that my boyfriend's recent lunch date, Stacie Meyers, was one of those girls. I glance at my phone. U awake? I'm home. Last band sucked. I knew he wouldn't stay until close. How is he going to work at Rafferty's? I call instead of texting.

"Hey," he says. "What are you doing up?"

That's the question of the night, isn't it? "Couldn't sleep."

"Insomnia-inducing fantasies about me again?"

"Always."

"Was I naked?"

"Except for the cape and red leather Vans." I picture his skinny legs in that getup and have to stifle a laugh.

"What time you working tomorrow?" Andrew asks.

"Three 'til close."

"Want to bike down to Island Beach State Park in the morning? Check out the osprey nests and the lighthouse?"

The ospreys return to their nests in Island Beach Park every year right about this time. They're like celebrities. There's an osprey cam and everything. The male arrives first and performs this cool ritual called a sky dance over the nest. Once the female arrives, the courtship begins and the male takes charge of feeding her. I guess he knows the way to her heart is through her stomach. Like me, ospreys must be part Italian.

"Won't you be tired?" I ask.

"Won't you?"

"Probably, but you know I'll be up early anyway," I say.

"Good. Wake me when you're on your way."

"Okay. I'll bring you coffee."

"And a lightly buttered bagel?" Andrew asks sweetly.

"And a lightly buttered bagel."

"Luce?"

"Yeah?"

"I missed you tonight. I wish you'd come with."

"Me too," I say, and I mean it.

Maybe I would have been better off never knowing my brother ruined whatever was between me and Connor. Then I wouldn't feel so guilty for wondering what that something was and whether or not Connor is even worth it.

Chapter 10

"Devotion to the nest more than their partner keeps ospreys together. They love where they live, not who they live with."

From "What's Love Got to Do with It? The Dating and Mating Habits of North American Sea Life." A junior thesis by Lucy Giordano.

The next morning I arrive at Andrew's house determined to be the old Lucy and forget about Connor and the kiss that almost happened last night. I step onto the wrap-around porch balancing a 7-Eleven cup holder with Andrew's coffee, my orange juice, and two tightly wrapped bagels, and breathe in the petunias and begonias in hanging baskets. During the storm, the Clarks' basement flooded with about two feet of bay water, which destroyed the hot water heater, boiler, washer and dryer, and some insulation. They also lost some baby toys and clothes that were in storage, but everything above the fourth basement stair remained unscathed.

Mrs. Clark sees me coming and rushes to hold open the screen door. She looks down at the food and shakes her head.

"You spoil him."

"I do."

"I heard that," Andrew yells from the top of the stairs.

You almost kissed Connor! my conscience screams. *You don't deserve him.*

I follow Mrs. Clark into the kitchen and put the food and drinks on the counter, inhaling the familiar smell of their home. It's like the bay meets Yankee Candles meets Mrs. Clark's flowery perfume. I've spent even more time here than usual lately. The Clarks moved back home in January, as soon as the water and power were restored. I love Gram, but it was nice to take the bus home with Andrew a couple of times a week. It made a weird time more normal.

Andrew comes flying down the steps seconds later, wraps his arms around me from behind, shakes his wet, wavy hair at me, and plants a kiss on my cheek.

"Andrew," I whine. I blush and break free. "I need a paper towel."

Mrs. Clark shakes her head at her son and hands me one. I'm still not used to being affectionate in front of her or Mr. Clark. They're like second parents to me and I don't want them picturing what her son and I are doing together, which isn't all that much, but still. I dry off my cheek as Andrew takes big bites of bagel and sips his coffee. He eats fast—and a lot for such a skinny dude.

"Go ahead, wipe away my kisses," he says, getting all mock sulky.

I laugh and crack open my juice. "More like your strawberry-scented shampoo. Very manly."

"I used Izzy's by mistake. Where's the little rug rat anyway?"

"Softball practice with your dad," Mrs. Clark says.

Andrew's little sister, Izzy, is ten. She has the same green eyes and wavy, dark-brown hair as Andrew, with a similar freckle pattern across her nose. Unlike me and Liam, there's no denying the resemblance between those two. Whenever I can, I stop by Izzy's room, tricked out with a canopy bed and plenty of pink, to get my Barbie and American Girl doll fix. She's like the little sister I never had. What if I could never hang out over here again? The orange juice burns in my empty stomach. If I lost Andrew, I'd lose the Clarks too.

Andrew finishes his bagel and grabs his coffee. No need to ask how he'll drink and ride at the same time. I've seen him do it plenty of times.

"Meet you out front," he says.

I grab my untouched bagel and put the cap back on my juice. "Bye, Mrs. Clark," I say.

"We'll see you tomorrow, right? Your parents and Liam are welcome too."

Andrew's parents are having their annual Memorial Day barbecue. I've always envied Andrew's parents' fun-loving ways. They seem happiest surrounded by a houseful of people. Not a holiday goes by without the Clarks marking it in some way. There are no annual anythings at our house. Maybe all those years of throwing a double birthday party every July wore out my parents. Or maybe my mom has simply lived in our house for too many years. It's the place where she grew up, so the tendency to keep to herself is ingrained.

I'm not sure what Dad's excuse is, other than he married Mom. He's a semi-Benny himself. His parents rented the same house every summer for something like twenty years. It's down the street from where we live, on the bayside. Dad's family would trudge up the block toward the beach with Wonder Wheelers laden with chairs, umbrellas, and towels. Dad said he would often see Mom on the front porch, reading a book or waxing her board. On one of those days, when my parents were both fifteen, Dad says he finally had the nerve to say "hello." Fast forward x number of years, and here Liam and I am.

"We'll be here," I say to Mrs. Clark. "I wouldn't miss it."

There's a line of cars at the entrance to Island Beach State Park waiting to pay the daily fee. They charge per vehicle, but walkers and bikers get in for free. We circumvent the line, which isn't all that terrible considering it's the Sunday before Memorial Day, and ride into the park to begin our long, straight ride.

About two miles down the road I pass a red fox sitting right under the fox crossing sign. They know how to work the crowd. I slow down and stop a safe distance from her. That's when I see three pups in the bushes behind her. Fluffy balls of cute.

"Look!" I shout to Andrew who's pedaling toward me, no hands, while sipping his coffee.

"Mama's showing her babes the ropes," Andrew says. He rolls closer and stops. Then he changes his voice to what I assume is his mother fox imitation. *"Sit up straight. Let 'em see your sad, wittle fox faces. That's right, stare into their cameras and look hungry."* Andrew again shakes his head. "These guys are not going to know how to hunt."

He's right. I'm guilty of feeding Scuttle, but he's just one bird. I don't interfere with the rest of the natural world on the island. Especially the foxes. These guys have got to learn how to hunt for food. In the winter, Island Beach State Park hardly gets any visitors aside from the hard-core fisher people.

"Come on," I say. "Let's keep going."

It's a ten-mile ride to the end of the park and this particular barrier island. In all, New Jersey has eleven barrier islands and about a hundred and thirty miles of beachfront from Sandy Hook to Cape May.

Farther down the road on our left, we bike past the two swimming beaches, which have lifeguards, bathrooms, and snack bars. Various trails shoot off the main road in either direction. The ones on our right lead to the bay, on the left, to the ocean. You can't see either body of water from the road because the thicket of vines, trees, and bushes is too dense.

"Is Papa Giordano working today?" Andrew asks as we pass the boat launch to Sedge Island. My dad works there every summer for the Division of Fish and Wildlife, and this year

I'm hoping to join him. I've already sent in my application for a Sedge Island internship.

I shake my head. "Not until school gets out in June."

We finally reach the island's tip, get off our bikes, and push them along the sand road that gives beach access to all-terrain vehicles, but it's too hard.

"Feels…like…I'm…on…a…treadmill…" Andrew exaggerates.

"Let's put our bikes over there." I point to a secluded path between thick shrubs. As I push my bike in that direction, I can smell the sweet fragrance of blooming beach plums and berry bushes mingling with pine. When Andrew pulls up beside me, our arms touch and I realize we're alone, which doesn't happen very often. I put my hand on his bicep, and he raises one eyebrow. I will my heart to do a couple of jumping jacks, to feel not as much as I did last night, but more than I do at this moment. We *are* good together. Normal. Familiar, from the Latin for *family*. That's what Andrew and I have the potential to become, right? If I don't believe that, then maybe I need to let him go. He puts both hands on my waist and draws me close before slipping his fingertips into my back pockets.

"We're not going to have time to see the osprey nests," I say when we finally pull apart.

"Screw the ospreys."

"What about the lighthouse?"

He looks behind him and considers it, which makes me wistful. We'd have to continue down the sandy road to the tip of the island, then walk toward the bay to see Barnegat

Lighthouse, which is on the barrier island south of here. What does it say about us that a long walk to see Old Barney is preferable to some alone time? Andrew scratches his chin and pretends to think.

"To the lighthouse!" he declares and takes off striding down the sand road. "Like how I did that?"

I jog to catch up. "Virginia Woolf would be proud."

Andrew's doing his junior thesis on *Mrs. Dalloway*, *A Room of One's Own*, and of course, *To the Lighthouse*. No student in the history of our high school has ever tackled those works before. But that's Andrew for you. He thinks it's funny that his paper will present both a challenge to him and our teacher, Ms. Stouffer, who will be forced to brush up on Virginia Woolf.

At times, Andrew's mildly irreverent brand of humor gets him in trouble. Like this past fall, when we were studying Shakespeare's sonnets and had to write our own. Andrew wrote his about prophylactics in perfect iambic pentameter. Irrespective of his gift for rhyme, Ms. Stouffer told him to either redo it and make it about love, or face a failing grade.

We reach the end of the road and walk along the western shore where the bay meets the Atlantic, so we can see the lighthouse. There are lots of boats out today. Red and green channel markers direct the traffic. Boats returning from the ocean are supposed to keep the red buoys to the starboard side of the boat. "Red, right, returning," the saying goes. Conversely, boaters keep green markers on the right side if they're headed from the bay to open water. I learned that from the Clarks, who taught me everything I know about boating, including how to water ski.

Near the bay's mouth, I spot a channel marker with both colors.

"What does it mean when a buoy is red and green?" I ask.

"That's a preferred channel marker. It's like a junction."

"So which way do you go?"

"You have to choose," Andrew says. "But one channel is still better than the other."

"How can you tell?" I ask.

"The preferred one is on top," he says.

"So if one is clearly better than the other, why give people a choice?"

Andrew shrugs, then puts his hands on my waist and gives me a quick kiss on the lips. "I guess because either way is fine."

"Sounds very 'Road Not Taken.'" Only in this case, one way *is* better. "I suppose you just need to make a decision."

"Yup. Unless you want to crash into the buoy."

Chapter 11

"Starfish can detach their arms to protect themselves against predators. The loss presents a unique opportunity for asexual reproduction. Not only can the starfish re-grow its missing arm, but a completely new starfish can form from the detached limb. Talk about a fresh start."

From "What's Love Got to Do with It? The Dating and Mating Habits of North American Sea Life." A junior thesis by Lucy Giordano.

All afternoon, I'm distracted at work. I almost hand out the wrong change twice and forget to give one eat-in customer—a mom and three kids—her number. Nothing disastrous, but it's so not me. I'd like to say it's from lack of sleep, but that's only half of it. The other half has to do with Connor. I keep thinking he's going to walk in any minute. Is that what I want? Andrew and I had fun this morning. Why isn't that enough? Why does my stomach twist every time I think about almost kissing Connor and my argument with Liam? This is why I prefer mornings. Crappy stuff seems to happen after midnight. Or maybe it all just looks crappier in the dark.

"How's day two on the register going, kiddo?" Adela asks and I jump. I didn't hear her come up behind me.

"Good. Great!"

"Everything okay? You don't seem like your smiley self today."

"Late night last night."

Adela crosses her arms and gives me a hard stare. "Don't let me find out our sweet Lucia has been drinking on the dunes."

"Pulease," Kiki chimes in. She's working the takeout register today. I've been so distracted that I just notice her bangs are green. "Saint Lucia, you mean? I'm surprised she gets sprinkles on her ice-cream cone. She's never even sipped a beer."

"I didn't think so," Adela says.

"Just insomnia, I guess. After working on my paper, I couldn't fall asleep."

"If it happens again, drink warm milk," Adela says as she walks away.

"Come on, does that really work?" Kiki asks.

"I know, right?" I say.

"You should look it up," Kiki suggests.

I would, but I'm hoping consulting the Internet regarding warm milk and insomnia won't be necessary. I don't need dairy; I need closure. Connor goes home tomorrow and that should end my sleepless nights for a while. I can go back to living life in my barrier-island bubble. At least until prom weekend, which unfortunately coincides with Bryn's. I'll have to face Connor then and again at the end of June when he'll be back for the summer. *If* he's coming back for the entire summer.

Maybe he'll get a job up north. Or maybe he'll return with Bryn. *Why do I care?*

"Uh, Luce?" Kiki asks.

"Yeah?"

"Why are you shredding those napkins?"

I look down at the counter. I've created a fluffy pile. "Whoops!" Quickly, I use both hands to gather the bits and toss them into the trash can under the register. "Just thinking about all the work I've got to do on my thesis."

"Nerd," Kiki teases before she answers the phone.

We get super busy during the dinner hour, leaving me no time to think or obsess, which is fine by me. At six thirty when I go on break, I grab a soft-shell chicken taco and an iced tea to go, walk up to the boardwalk, and find an empty bench. I love this time of day, right before twilight. The shadows grow long and the sun hangs over the bay, waiting to turn the sky pink and purple. There's just the right amount of chill in the air. I zip my hoodie and watch the lingering beachgoers, their cheeks flushed from the sun, pull sweatshirts and cover-ups over their bathing suits before heading to their cars.

I finish my dinner and walk south—away from my Victorian dream house. The mere thought of seeing it still rattles me. I avert my eyes whenever I go by, which upsets me on a deeper level. I can't have Connor messing up everything I love about this place. *I'm* the one who lives here.

A sharp easterly wind sweeps across the boardwalk, making it feel ten degrees colder. Even at the height of summer, when the humidity is up around ninety-five percent, the breeze that comes off the ocean can make crossing the dunes feel like stepping out of the desert and into the frozen dessert aisle at ShopRite. My phone rings as I cross the street on my way back to work.

"Where are you?" Kiki demands when I answer.

"Walking back from break, why?"

"Connor Malloy came in for takeout." She says it like it's big news.

"And? Should I take to social media and let the world know?"

"He was asking for you."

My stomach does a burpee. "Probably just wanted to say 'hey.'"

"Mmm-hmm." Her suspicious tone makes my pulse race.

"What? We're neighbors."

"He didn't look very neighborly."

"What's that supposed to mean?"

"I dunno. He looked worried. Like he really needed to see you."

"So?"

"So, I know that look. Is there something going on?"

"What? Me and Connor Malloy? Keeks, how could you say that? I'm with Andrew!"

"I know. I just…"

"Just what?"

"Luce, I'm not blind. We've been friends since pre-K, and whenever Connor's around, you always get that look on your face."

"What look?"

"Like a kid who really wants a cookie but was told she can't have one."

"And what does that look like exactly?"

"Like Connor when I told him you were on a break."

I nearly drop my phone. I don't dare ask Kiki, but instead imagine Connor's urgent expression. I allow hope to creep into my chest and warm the icy bitterness that collected there all winter. Then I push it all away and stick to my story.

"I am not Connor's forbidden cookie and he's not mine. Anyway, he's with that girl now. Brook or Britta or Bryn."

"He wasn't today."

"Keeks. What are you trying to say?"

"Did something happen with Connor?"

I stop walking in the middle of the sidewalk. *Does she know? How could she?* No one knows. She'd never talk to me again if she found out I kept the whole thing a secret. Had it turned into something real, I would have told Kiki and Meghan about my morning with Connor, but the way it all fell apart was humiliating. I just wanted to forget, and no one else knowing made that easier. Or so I thought.

"Are you kidding? Me and Connor? We are so not right for each other. He's a dog. Plus, let me repeat, I'm with Andrew."

"I know. Just checking. I totally agree that Connor's all wrong for you. You and Andrew are perfect. I just wanted to hear you say it."

Keeks doesn't hide the fact that she's the product of a

summer fling. Watching her mom work so hard to raise her alone has made Kiki acutely wary of outsiders.

"You sound like Liam."

"I knew there was a reason I loved that boy."

She also doesn't hide her affection for Liam.

"Okay then," I say. "I'm rounding the corner now. I'll see you in about thirty seconds."

"No, you won't. I left for the day. That's why I *called*."

That's right. I forgot Kiki was already there when I came in at three today. I'm relieved no one at Breakwater Burrito overheard her side of the conversation.

"Thanks for the heads-up, Keeks. Talk later."

"Luce?"

"Yeah?"

"You know you can tell me anything, right?"

Oh boy. "Of course."

"Good." Then she makes a kissing noise into the phone, says "later," and hangs up.

My left eye is twitching. Why is my left eye twitching? Because I'm a big, fat liar, that's why. A big, fat liar who needs a jelly doughnut and a Yoo-hoo to help calm her down before she goes back to work. I still have five minutes so I stop at White Oak Market to buy both. I'm at the register, about to start telling the cashier, Trevor, all about how Yoo-hoo was invented in New Jersey in the 1920s, when I notice a petition on the counter, next to a collection jar for the Seaside Park Education Fund.

"What's that?" I ask Trevor.

"Petition asking the governor to lift the ban on child labor and allow teens to help with the rebuilding."

"Can I sign it?"

Trevor hands me a pen. "Knock yourself out."

"Thanks." I flip through the pages, looking for an empty line to put my name, address, email, and signature. I'm about to sign, but as I skim the petition, I realize that I can't and hand the pen back to Trevor.

"Changed your mind?"

"I've got to be eighteen and a registered voter."

"Bummer. Well, you can still help rebuild if the law gets changed."

"I guess I can."

I've been so focused on my thesis and getting that internship on Sedge Island that I hadn't considered helping out more with the Superstorm Sandy recovery. I scan the list for names I recognize. Not surprisingly there are lots. Trevor has signed, and so have my Breakwater Burrito bosses. The Harrisons, who live across the street from us, and Jim Malloy, Connor's father. He's a contractor, so it makes sense. I wonder if his company is donating labor. Underneath Jim Malloy's name is Connor's. Figures. He doesn't want to be with me and yet I can't seem to get away from him. "Dammit!"

"Everything okay there, Luce?"

"What? Oh yeah. Stubbed my toe."

As I leave the market and head back to work, I've determined the petition is a sign from the gods. It's the opening I need to get closure. I'm going to mention it to Connor. Tell him he needs to be eighteen to sign it. He probably didn't read the whole thing. I may even ask about whether his dad's helping out with the rebuild.

It's not just an excuse, I tell myself. It's a better conversation starter than: "We need to talk." *Right?* Connor and I have to get back to being nothing more than neighbors—and part-time neighbors at that. I want to move forward with Andrew, but I need to clear the path of Connor first. Because right now, I fear I'm on a crash course with a buoy.

Chapter 12

"Hermit crabs mate in the ocean but live on land. The journey from fertilization to home ownership is a quick one for these creatures. In just four months, a juvenile hermit crab moves into its first home. And once a hermit crab reaches sexual maturity, it is nearly impossible to remove it from the shell in which it lives."

From "What's Love Got to Do with It? The Dating and Mating Habits of North American Sea Life." A junior thesis by Lucy Giordano.

My parents are shouting at each other upstairs when I walk through the front door and into our living room, which overshadows my joy that Mom finally got the flat-screen TV mounted in place. My parents *never* fight—not like this. I creep halfway up the steps and listen. They're so loud that I wouldn't even call what I'm doing eavesdropping.

"It's just one year. Possibly just one summer, if we move fast enough," Dad says.

"I'm not renting our home to strangers."

"We may have to *sell* our home to strangers if we don't."

"We'll cut back in other ways. Sell one car. Nix the November trip." Mom's voice is softer now.

We always jet off to some cool location during the first week of November—California, the Bahamas, Disney World. Schools in New Jersey have a fall break, and since my parents need to work summer jobs, it's a good time for us to travel. My hometown may be small, but I've been all over this country and still haven't found a place I love as much.

"I don't think that'll be enough," Dad says.

"The cottage will be done by next summer."

"The kids will be starting college after next summer."

"I don't want to talk about this anymore," Mom says. "I'm not leaving our home." I hear their door open, then scamper down the stairs into the kitchen, where I throw open the refrigerator and stare into it, acting like I've been there this whole time.

Mom jumps when she sees me. "Oh, honey! I didn't hear you come in. Are you hungry? There's leftover pasta. I figured you ate at work."

"I did. Just thirsty." I take out a bottle of water and crack open the top. I don't want to pretend I don't know what's going on. My adrenaline's pumping too hard to just let it go. "I heard what Dad said. He wants us to leave? We just got back. I don't want people I don't know sleeping in my room."

Mom's still wearing her lifeguard sweat suit. Her dark blond hair is pulled back into a twist. Usually, she looks more like she's in her thirties than her forties, but tonight she looks tired. "I know, hon," Mom says. "Your father's just stressed. He'll calm down. The meeting with the contractor didn't go so well yesterday. Rebuilding the rental cottage is going to cost more than we thought."

"Maybe you should talk to Mr. Malloy. He's a contractor and…"

But Mom just waves me off, a frustrating move that forces me to change tactics and try to come up with another solution. It's scary to think we might not be able to afford rebuilding the cottage or staying in our home. "Use my college money for the contractor. I can take out loans. Maybe I'll get a scholarship. We can't leave again." I'm about to cry and can't hide it.

Mom opens her arms. "Come here."

I let her give me a big hug, one that feels long overdue. She rests her chin on top of my head, and I let myself cry about *everything*—not just the possibility of us leaving here. Maybe I should tell her about Connor. She might understand. More and more, I feel like I need to tell someone.

"We're not going to touch your college money. The remodel has added value to this house. We can take out a line of credit, or maybe sell and downsize."

"Downsize? So we still might have to leave?"

"Better to leave the house than to leave altogether, right?"

I'm not so sure about that. I bite my bottom lip and don't say anything. Now's not the time to bring up the misadventures of Lucy Giordano and the boy next door.

"Let me and Dad worry about this, okay?" Mom says.

Seriously? Of course I'll worry. It sucks that we had to

temporarily relocate to Gram's. I can't imagine leaving forever. This house is part of us. Well, I can't speak for my entire family, especially Liam who talks more and more about how much he wants to leave, but this house is part of *me*. I love my room. My partial ocean view. The people on my block. I belong on this island for sure, but more than that, I belong in this house.

I take a step back from our hug and look Mom in the eye. "Do Liam and I get a say? Can we have a family meeting about this?"

Mom sighs. "You know we'll listen to whatever you and Liam have to say. But as much as I want us all to be happy, we may have to make some sacrifices. Understand?"

I nod, and Mom gives me one last hug before she turns and goes upstairs. I wipe my eyes, walk out onto the screened-in porch, and flop down on the rattan sofa. I glance at the hurricane lamp in the center of the coffee table. Normally, I like to burn candles out here, especially honeysuckle-scented ones. But after spending a week in the dark at Gram's house post-hurricane, the smell of lit candles makes me sick. So does just thinking about how that one storm, that one day, changed everything.

·· ● ··

Connor held my hands as we stood on the porch of the old house, and I could hear the *clang, clang, clang* of the flagpole's hook. The wind was already strong enough to blow sand from the dunes onto Ocean Avenue. The tiny grains hissed as they skittered across the pavement.

"Be safe, Luce," he said. His eyes lingered on my face before he kissed me. If I had known it was going to be the last time, I wouldn't have been the first to pull away. But I had to get home, and the longer we kissed, the harder it was to stop. When we did, I wrapped my arms around his neck and nuzzled my face against his neck. He held me tight and whispered in my ear: "I'll call you as soon as I can, okay? I promise." He didn't have to promise. I could hear it in his voice.

I made one quick detour before going home, and when I finally got back to my house—much later than I intended—I was swept into the chaotic swirl of activity. Mom cast an annoyed glance my way as she placed boxes into the trunk of her Nissan. Dad, who was putting the bike rack on the car, barked at me to hurry up and pack. I parked Misty next to his Jeep, then ran up to my room and frantically gathered what I wanted to bring. An hour later, I came downstairs with a suitcase, a duffel bag, and my school backpack.

I'd whittled down my precious items to the things I would hate to lose—the white-gold starfish necklace I got for my sixteenth birthday, a well-worn copy of *A Field Guide to North Atlantic Wildlife: Marine Mammals, Seabirds, Fish, and Other Sea Life*, and my fully charged laptop so I could work on my sea-life dating-mating thesis. I also brought Frenchie, the stuffed poodle I've had since kindergarten, and the pillows and quilt from my bed—the things I can't sleep without.

Liam was sitting on the couch with his guitar and one small bag. He scowled at me when he saw what I was bringing.

"What?" I said.

"You're overacting, as usual," he said.

"And you're just too cool to give a crap," I snapped. "As usual."

My father had just walked into the living room. "Hey, hey, hey. Enough. Get your stuff in the car and let's get out of here."

"But we have until four o'clock," Liam moaned.

"Move," Dad said. "I want to gas up both cars and leave before the last-minute rush."

Normally, the drive to Gram's is only fifteen minutes, but there was a lot of traffic on the bridge and we didn't get there until mid-afternoon. Gram was cooking chicken cutlets and a baked ziti in her electric stove. It was our last hot meal for a while. After that, we ate lots of bagels and PB&J.

By late afternoon, we were all on Gram's couch, staring at the Doppler radar on TV as that enormous green mass with its mammoth-sized red eye crept up the Eastern Seaboard like a slow-moving monster. The news anchors and weathermen were throwing around terms like "epic" and "hundred-year" to describe the approaching storm. All we could do was sit there like lobsters in the tank at the Seafood Shanty, waiting for Superstorm Sandy to unleash her prolonged wrath—torrential rains, surging waters, and seventy-five-mile-an-hour sustained winds that sounded like jumbo jets splitting the air space directly above the roof.

I remember the mixture of fear and resolve on Mom's face when the lights went out shortly after five—and stayed off for the next seven days. "This is it," she said as she stood up, took the glass off the hurricane lamp, and lit the flame.

· • ● •• ·

"Why are you sitting in the dark?" Connor's voice comes through the open porch window, and I fly into the sitting position, banging my knee on the glass coffee table in the process.

"Jesus, Connor. You scared the crap out of me." I twist my body so I'm facing him.

"Sorry, Luce. You okay in there? Sounds like you hurt something." Connor cups his hands around his eyes and squints through the screen directly behind the couch, where I'd been lying down until he scared the bejesus out of me.

"I'm fine. I was going to come see you."

"You were?" Connor sounds surprised.

I nod, though I'm not sure he can see me. "I saw you signed the petition at the White Oak. Did you know you have to be eighteen?"

"I am eighteen," Connor says. "I got redshirted in kindergarten. I was the youngest and smallest in the class, and my parents thought I needed another year of cutting and pasting."

Connor is close to six foot now and built more like a man than a boy so I guess it all worked out okay.

"Oh," I say, forgetting this was my opening for closure.

"I'm hoping the law gets changed, but I'm still old enough to volunteer with the rebuild this summer, which is my plan."

"So you'll be coming back in June?"

"Right after school lets out."

"Where's Bryn?" I keep my tone even.

"Taking a shower. We're going to her friend's party in Toms River."

"Sounds fun." It doesn't, but I don't know what else to say.

"It's kind of weird talking to you through the screen. It's like I'm at old-time confession."

I've seen Connor at church on Sundays but didn't take him for a hardcore Catholic. "Spend a lot of time looking for forgiveness, do you?" I joke.

Connor laughs. "Not enough. Can I come in?"

I'm not sure if Liam's home. Forget Liam—what about me? What do I want? "Probably not a good idea."

"Please? I need to talk to you."

I adjust myself so now I'm cross-legged facing him, the shadowy figure with shimmery blue eyes hovering in the window above the couch. Smoke from the neighbor's barbecue drifts into the yard, making me think it would be a nice night to light the chiminea. "I can hear you just fine."

"I want to see you."

I want to see him too. "Walk over to the door."

"You're letting me in?"

"No. I'm letting you stand by the door."

I get off the couch and open the screen door a crack. Enough to see Connor's entire face.

"You sure know how to make a guy feel welcome," he says when he reaches the top step.

"What did you want to talk about?"

"About us…being friends. Can we do that?"

I don't know who he's asking. Himself or me. It's exactly what I wanted to talk to *him* about, so why don't I just say "yes" and be done with it? Because when he's this close to me, I can feel his fingertips caressing my face, the way his muscles contracted as I ran my hands along his abs, his chest, his back…

"Luce?"

"What?"

"Friends?"

"We *are* friends." Something in my voice gives me away.

"But then we were more," he finishes.

There it is. The acknowledgment I've been waiting for since October twenty-eighth. I give him a half smile and try not to crumble.

"We were, right?" I whisper.

"*Luce.*" He says my name with a mixture of tenderness and hurt. Tears prick my eyes, and I have to swallow back the lump in my throat.

He reaches for my face, but I back away.

"Luce…" he says again, softer this time. "Bryn's prom is…"

I shake my head. "Andrew—" I begin, then break off. I can't talk.

Connor nods quickly, like he doesn't want me to finish anyway. I take a deep breath.

"Friends?" Connor says again and puts out his hand.

I open the door a bit wider and place my hand in his. There's warmth between us that I've never felt with anyone else. I never want to let go, and that's why I have to.

"Friends," I say. It's more like a wish than a statement.

"So…" He doesn't move his hand or drop his eyes, and neither do I.

"So."

"You and Drew should come to this party with us."

Worst. Idea. Ever. "Quit the crazy talk."

"What? It's what friends do. Go to parties together. Double date."

I finally let my hand drop. "Connor, I just got off work. I haven't showered. I'm not even sure Andrew would go."

"Call him. Shower. I'll bet you're ready before Bryn fires up the flat iron." He walks down the steps and my heart lurches. *Don't go.*

I start to follow him, and we nearly collide when he turns back. "Connor, wait. I can't… I'm not going anywhere. I'm sorry."

He reaches out, then pulls his hand away. "I know." He turns but calls over his shoulder as he nears the edge of the yard, "Let me know if you change your mind."

If only it were that easy.

Chapter 13

"Albatross courtships include an intricate, beautiful mating dance. The birds spread their wings, clack their beaks together, and let out a long, honking call. Once the ritual is complete and the mates chose each other, it really is 'until death do us part.'"

From "What's Love Got to Do with It? The Dating and Mating Habits of North American Sea Life." A junior thesis by Lucy Giordano.

I don't see Connor again until the night of the junior prom. In the three weeks since we've shared the same geography, thousands of adult clams have completed their broadcast spawning cycle, which is like sex without attachment, literally, and a whole new batch of seed clams have settled into the sediment of the bay, ready to be retrieved and begin protected life in an upweller. By October, they'll have grown into adults without having to endure such complicated coming-of-age rituals as proms and prom *pictures*.

Connor pulls up with Bryn just as we're wrapping up the interminable photo shoot at my house, and the feelings I thought I'd learned to control come flooding back like the lunar tide cycle. I was so over taking pictures fifteen minutes ago. Now I really want to just get the hell out of here already. We've already had similar picture-taking sessions at Meghan's house, where the limo picked us up, and Kiki's. To save time (yeah, right), the guys' parents met us at my house. My own parents are among the guys' group since, surprisingly, my barely communicative brother stepped up and offered to be Kiki's date when hers—some dude she met at the mall food court—flaked.

Liam heard me on the phone a week ago as I sat at our new breakfast bar asking Andrew's opinion about a replacement date for Keeks. When I got off the phone, Liam looked at me and said, "I'll go with Kiki. If you think she'd want that." *Would Kiki want that? It's like her dream come true!* But I played it all nonchalant, for Keeks's sake as well as my own. My brother has been cold to me since our fight over Memorial Day weekend, and I didn't want him to know how awesome I thought he was being. "I'll check," I told him. And here we all are.

"You look so hot in that dress," Andrew whispers in my ear before my parents snap our picture. I'm wearing a floor-length, pale-blue halter with ballet flats, since even a slight heel would make me taller than Andrew. My hair's down in soft, wavy curls—a "natural" look that took Kiki's stylist more than an hour to accomplish. Keeks insisted we all pay to have our hair and makeup done. My eyes are so glammed up that they don't close all the way. I'm used to being the smartest, not the prettiest girl in the pack, but I do have my moments. I think tonight is one of them. I feel so amazing that I'm even standing straighter.

Andrew's adorableness is at an all-time high. He found this vintage tux at a thrift shop. I liked how it looked in all black and told him not to bother matching his bow tie to my ensemble. Tonight he's wearing the tux with black Converse high tops, and his hair has been tamed with some product—the whole look makes me want to hug him. He smells nice too, more like a Hollister guy and less like he had mistakenly used Izzy's shampoo again.

"Kiki and Liam, you two are next," Mom orders. We finished the group shots, and now the parents want one of each couple. The junior prom will be over and Connor and Bryn will be engaged by the time we leave here.

Kiki is wearing a short, pink dress with a sparkly bodice and full skirt. I don't know how her stylist managed it, but Kiki's bangs are the exact same shade as her dress. I can't believe Liam didn't bail when he found out he'd be wearing a matching pink tie and vest. *They look so good together*, I think, as I frame a shot with my phone. They're both so darned attractive that they could model prom wear for *Teen Vogue*.

"Meghan! You're next!" shouts Mom. Sometimes she forgets she's not at work and we're not her lifeguard minions.

Meghan's shimmery floral print gown is long like mine, and Mateo is wearing a classic black-and-white tux. As the parental paparazzi take pics of Meghan and Mateo, I force myself to focus on my friends and not Connor's house, but he's walking back and forth between the side door and his truck, unloading God knows what. He must've made five trips already. So I smile, stand tall in my gown, and pretend to hang on Kiki's every word while I wait for the driver to start the car and open the limo door so we can go.

Finally the engine turns over. I give my parents a quick hug, promise not to stay out too late, and hustle toward the idling white stretch limo. Next thing I know, I hear Andrew call Connor's name. My breath catches in my throat. *Why is my boyfriend talking to Connor?*

I sneak a look as I slide across the backseat. Even a quick glimpse of his profile makes my heart double pump. Connor shrugs, says something I can't hear, then puts up one hand and yells to Andrew: "Have fun!"

Andrew's the last one to get into the backseat, because of his conversation with his new best friend. Mateo and Liam sit facing us girls. Andrew winds up next to Kiki, farthest from me, which would be fine if he didn't decide to talk to me about Connor with Kiki and Meghan in between.

"You should have seen the look on Connor's face when I asked him if his girlfriend was moving in." Andrew laughs. "She had a ton of crap."

"You should have seen the look on his face when he saw you in that dress," Meghan whispers so only I can hear.

"Yeah?" I say to Andrew. I'm afraid to look at either Meghan or my brother right now. Meghan and I have never really talked much about Connor, except to acknowledge his obvious good looks. Liam and I haven't mentioned Connor since that night he told me about the alleged Natalie-Connor hook up. Our communication has been limited to the mundane. What's Dad cooking for dinner? How much do I owe you for the limo? Are the Mets losing again? Things between us have been so icy that I was hoping tonight could begin the thaw. But not if Andrew keeps talking about Connor.

I need to take the chitchat in another direction. "What time did Mom say we need to be home?" I ask Liam.

"One," he says. "We can probably make it more like two or three if you ask."

Interesting. I didn't think he'd want his night with Keeks to last that long. "Why me?"

"Because it'll sound better coming from you. She won't think we're up to something."

"Will we be up to something?" Kiki wiggles her eyebrows.

"There's an after-party at Ryan's," Mateo says.

Ugh. I don't want to go to a party and hang out with a bunch of well-dressed drunks.

"Rafferty's is doing an all-ages show. Some indie band from Atlanta is headlining," Andrew adds. "I heard they're really good." He hasn't been working there that long, and already I'm a little sick of hearing about it.

How about just building a fire at Andrew's and making s'mores like we used to? I'd like to say. *Anyone?*

Predictably Liam is all over the Rafferty's idea.

"Let's do it then." Kiki beams. She's so in love with my brother that she'd play post-prom paintball if that's what he wanted to do. Liam better not break her heart.

The limo's just pulling into the high-school parking lot when my phone vibrates in my purse. I'm guessing it's Mom because everyone else I know is here. Andrew helps both Kiki and Meghan out of the car before taking my hand as I exit the limo. Maneuvering in a floor-length gown isn't easy, even if I am wearing flats.

"Ready to go inside?" Andrew asks.

"Just a sec. I think my mom just texted me."

Liam hears me and yells, "Ask her about staying out later!"

Andrew's busy watching cars and limos stream into the parking lot. Plenty of kids drove, but a lot are getting dropped at the curb like us. The football team and their dates rented an entire party bus, which has captured Andrew's fascination. He walks over to take a closer look while I check my phone.

I unlock the screen and immediately see two words: You're beautiful. Actually, I don't see them as much as hear them. Connor said them to me once before. He's the only one who ever has. It's like he knew, *knows*, there's a big difference between being told "You *look* beautiful" for which a good hair day or the right lighting could be responsible, and "You are beautiful," which is so much more. His words make me remember his touch.

"What'd she want?" Andrew asks.

"What?" I clear my screen and shove my phone back in my bag.

"Your mom. What'd she want?"

"Oh. I left my lip gloss on the kitchen counter. No biggie. Not even sure why she texted."

"I think your lips look just fine," Andrew says, and kisses me before we walk through the front door. My skin is flushed, and I'm honestly not sure if it's because of the guy who just kissed me or the one who's thinking about me. And just why is he thinking about me when he's playing house for the weekend with Bryn? What happened to "friends"?

Inside we take even more pictures with a professional photographer before sitting down to a chicken dinner in the cafeteria-auditorium, which has been transformed by the deejay's lighting and two not-so Jumbotron screens. (I think they're actually SMART Boards.) Some sort of silky material has been draped from the ceiling and pinned to the walls. The effect is similar to walking into a nightclub inside a gold chiffon circus tent.

Meghan prods her food with a fork. "What's this chicken stuffed with anyway?"

"I believe it's more chicken," Andrew says.

Liam laughs. "Chicken-stuffed chicken." Andrew's one of the few people my bro finds funny, and yet somehow they never became good friends. I always figured Andrew wasn't edgy enough for Liam.

Kiki looks around and scowls. "I knew it. I should have joined the prom committee."

"What's the matter, Keeks? The decor not to your liking?" Andrew asks as his eyes pan the room. "I don't know. I kinda like watching Rihanna on one screen and Paulie Gantos stuffing potatoes au gratin into his mouth on the other."

Liam laughs again.

"I'm totally taking charge of our senior prom committee next year," Kiki says. "Who's with me?'

Meghan raises her hand, then looks at me. "What?" I say. "You guys know I'd be no help. Tell them, Andrew."

But my boyfriend and my brother have both been rendered speechless by the sight of Stacie Meyers floating our way across the dance floor. Her dress is so tight and so short that I'm expecting a pole to drop down from the ceiling any second. The look on Andrew's face makes me feel like I'm the chicken-stuffed chicken next to the only serving of filet mignon in the room.

Stacie walks right up to Andrew, wedging herself between my chair and his as if I'm wearing an invisibility cloak. "Hey, Andy," she croons.

Who the hell is Andy? That's what I'd like to know.

"Hey, Stacie," Andrew says. I can tell he wants to play it cool, but his voice cracks.

"Your hair looks good like that. I told you it would."

Wait, what? Stacie's telling my boyfriend how to dress now? Oh, I'd love to see Andrew's expression but can't because Stacie's ass is about two inches away from my face. I make a big display of moving my chair about a foot to the left and give Kiki and Meghan my WTF face. They oblige me by shooting evil glares at Stacie.

"A group of us are meeting backstage in five minutes," Stacie says.

"For what?" Andrew asks innocently.

"To party." She dangles her bag in front of Andrew's face like it contains magic beans. "No one would expect us to be behind the deejay. It's genius."

"Hiding in plain sight." Andrew grins and Stacie touches the tip of her nose twice. I don't like this. I don't like this one bit.

Andrew got the job at Rafferty's right after Memorial Day. It's more bar than restaurant, but they serve burger-type food and he and Stacie work a lot of the same shifts. I'd like to say I'm fine with it. That I don't get the least bit jealous when Andrew regales me with his latest hilarity from the Stacie Waitressing Chronicles. I can only hope Andrew's equally as enthusiastic when he tells Stacie about *me*.

"Bring your friends," Stacie says as she glances around the table. Her eyes linger on Liam, then Andrew, before she turns and walks away. Mateo's smart enough to put his arm around Meghan and kiss her cheek as Stacie struts back from whence she came. It's a move that says, *I'm not going anywhere, baby.* Maybe that's what soul mates do? Mateo gets it. Liam and Andrew do not. They look all too willing to trade what they've already won (Hello! Kiki and I are sitting right here!) for a look at the treasure inside Stacie's purse.

Andrew folds his napkin and places it alongside his plate, then pushes back from the table. "Luce? You mind if I cut out for a few?"

"You're not serious," I say to Andrew.

Andrew lowers his voice. "Come on, Luce. It's prom. No one is driving. Two shots of Jack won't turn me on to harder drugs. Swear." He puts his hand over his heart, thinking he's being funny. He's not.

"Oh for Chrissake, Luce," Liam butts in. "Can't you take a break from being your sanctimonious self for once? We'll be right back."

"Stay out of this, Liam," I say as Kiki rests her hand on my brother's elbow. "Besides, why can't Kiki and I join you?"

"Because last time I checked, you don't party," Liam retorts.

My jaw tightens and my body gets hot with rage. I push my chair away from the table, about to bolt for who knows where, when Andrew takes my hand. "Come with me, Luce. You're right. I should have invited you to begin with. I just didn't think you'd be interested."

Andrew's nervous. He should be. Going to the junior prom together was *his* idea. *He's* the one who decided it was time to turn all our years of best friendship into something more. So what now? He's going to ruin our night before it even gets started by sneaking off backstage to share a flask with Stacie and her friends. Andrew doesn't party either. That's what he should have said to Liam. And don't get me started on the germs. I know the alcohol will kill the germs, but other people's spit? Gross.

"Just go, Andrew. If that's what you want, I'm not going to stop you."

"You won't be mad?"

He can't be serious. *Tell him, Mateo*, I want to shout. When did my boyfriend become an idiot? I sense my mouth hanging open. I take a deep breath and exhale. "No. Go ahead. Liam'll keep an eye on you, I'm sure. Right, Liam?"

Liam pops out of his seat and puts a hand on Andrew's shoulder. "What'ya say, man?"

"Luce?" Andrew looks at me with sad Saint Bernard eyes.

"Just go."

"Thanks! We'll be right back. I swear."

"Take your time," I mumble as my brother and Andrew practically sprint off to find Stacie and her bag of tricks.

"I'm going to the ladies' room," Meghan says. "You coming with?" She looks more at me than Kiki.

"Yeah, sure. Why not?" I've got nothing better to do since my boyfriend chose what was behind curtain number one instead of me.

Kiki and I follow Meghan to the bathroom. Once the three of us are alone, she looks at me and says, "What're you guys thinking? Letting them go off with Stacie like that?"

"What was I supposed to do? You heard my brother. It's bad enough I could tell how much Andrew wanted to go, but then Liam had to get up in my face like that."

Kiki says nothing. She knows one date with my brother does not a relationship make. In fact, any chance she has would have been blown if she'd tried to stop him. Meghan shakes her head. "Mateo knows that if his butt moved even an inch off that chair, we'd be done."

"Mateo didn't look like he *wanted* to move off that chair," I point out.

"It wasn't always that way," Meghan says. "Boys need to be schooled when it comes to respect."

"But shouldn't Andrew want to stay with me on prom night?" I ask myself more than Meghan. We haven't even slowed-danced yet. "I remember that when you started dating Mateo, we never saw you anymore. You spent every second together. Isn't that the way it's supposed to be?"

A look of sympathy flashes across Meghan's face. "Every relationship is different. Mateo and I didn't start out as friends. There was no period of adjustment or transition," she says.

Meghan is wise to be so diplomatic. Love isn't math; there are no precise answers. It's more like chemistry, governed by tiny, fast-moving, unpredictable particles that somehow find a way to collide. Every couple is its own equation, its own chemical reaction. Asking Meghan what works for her and Mateo doesn't necessarily mean I'll find what will work for me and Andrew. Love, like chemistry, has too many moving parts and unknowns. Sex and reproduction? That's pure biology. Perhaps that's why I'm most drawn to a science with causes and effects I can predict and understand—at least in the animal kingdom. What's going to happen with Meghan and Mateo a year from now? What if they go to different colleges hundreds of miles apart? In science and in real life, I do know that successful unions depend on location.

· ● · ·

When we walk back into the cafeteria-auditorium, Mateo is still sitting all alone at our table. I was hoping Andrew would be back by now. I'm not expecting much from my brother, but for Kiki's sake, it would have been nice for him to be there too. My eyes pan the dance floor, but there's no sign of Andrew, Liam, or Stacie.

"I'll be right back," I say to Kiki and Meghan. I walk back into the hall and toward the stage's side entrance, the one that leads to the wings. It's too dark to see anything as I step through the door, but I immediately hear giggling. I close my eyes until they adjust to the blackness, then follow the voices coming from behind the curtain—the one that hides the stagehands during performances.

When I get there, it takes my brain a few seconds to understand what I'm seeing. Liam takes a long pull from a silver flask, then hands it to Stacie, who's sitting on Andrew, who's sitting on a prop box with his hand on Stacie's waist.

"Andrew?" I'm not loud. Not hysterical. Not even sure I can be heard. But everyone looks at me, so I know I was.

"Lucy!" Andrew jumps up so fast that he propels Stacie off his lap and into my brother, who catches her before she falls through the curtain. I turn on my heels and don't wait for excuses and explanations. I bust through the stage doors, and instead of running back down the hall toward the music, I duck into an empty classroom.

I wait until I hear the heavy stage door open and close. Wait for Andrew's footsteps to walk off in the wrong direction. Wait until I'm sure no one will think to look for me here. I take out my phone, open Connor's text, and hit Reply. Can u come and get me? I type. Then I start to cry.

Chapter 14

"Mating season can be rough on female sea otters. The polygynous males, an aggressive bunch of players, often bite their mates' noses, causing some unlucky ladies to bleed and leaving the unluckier still with lifelong scars."

From "What's Love Got to Do with It? The Dating and Mating Habits of North American Sea Life." A junior thesis by Lucy Giordano.

I clutch my phone, eyes fixed on the screen, waiting to see the ellipses in the bubble that mean Connor's typing a response. When I don't, I cry harder. I'm rummaging through the teacher's desk for tissues when my phone rings.

"Whereareyouareyouallright?" Connor's words bleed together like one long word.

I swallow the messy glob of tears and mucus collecting in my throat. "I'm fine. I'm at the high school. The prom."

"You're crying. What happened?" Connor's anxious voice is a hair above a whisper.

"Wait. Where are *you*?"

"At dinner. With Bryn."

"She's sitting right *there*?"

"I'm in the men's room. That's why it took me a few minutes to call. Are you in trouble? I can be there in fifteen minutes."

"No, Connor. I'm fine, really. I feel so stupid now. I shouldn't have texted you."

I give Connor the abbreviated version of the Andrew-Stacie lap-dance saga. I don't want him to keep his friends waiting.

"Guys can be stupid sometimes," Connor says. "Talk to him."

"I know what he'll say. He'll say they're just friends."

"Like me and you?"

"You're the one who suggested that's what we should be."

"You know what I mean."

I do. Hypocrite that I am, sitting here in this darkened classroom talking to Connor after I asked him to come pick me up.

"Talk to him," Connor says again.

"I will."

"And if you still want to go home, call me."

"What about Bryn?"

"Let me worry about Bryn."

"Connor?"

"Yeah?"

"Thank you."

"For what?"

"Calling. Calming me down…your text earlier."

"It was nothing."

"The text wasn't nothing. It was the best part of my night."

"It'll get better. I promise."

• • ● • •

I step into an unlocked and empty faculty bathroom and attempt to fix my smudged makeup before heading back to party central with DeeJay Tom. Kiki does a double take when I walk into the room. She nudges Meghan's arm and the pair rushes up to me. My best friends certainly know how to move in heels.

"Where've you been?" Meghan screams.

"We've been looking all over for you. Andrew's outside right now. He might need our help to get back in."

No one is allowed to reenter the building once they leave. Prom rules. *Serves him right*, I think. Suddenly, I don't want to see him. I don't want to hear that what I witnessed between him and Stacie was totally innocent. I *know* Andrew. Better than he knows himself, maybe. And I saw the way he looked at Stacie tonight. It's more than just tonight.

I can tell how he feels about her by the way he says her name. I can hear it in his voice, the underlying excitement that he's trying to control for my benefit. I know he anticipates her arrival at work. I sense the flip in his stomach when she walks through the door. I get it. That's how it's supposed to be when a crush turns into something more. The saddest part is that Andrew and I don't feel that way about each other. I don't know that we ever had the chance to. We are forever friends, kindred spirits even, but we are not soul mates.

"I need some water," I tell the girls, and they usher me over to our table, where Liam is sitting with Mateo.

"Way to overreact, Luce," Liam says.

"You're right, Liam. I'm sure if Natalie had been sitting in Andrew's lap, you would have let it roll off your back. Where is she, by the way?" I look around for effect. "I thought I saw her come in with Doug Balaczek."

Liam's cheeks flush red, and I wish I could take back what I said. Not for my brother—he deserves it. But for Kiki, who doesn't need to see how much my brother's ex still gets to him. I'm sipping my water when a disheveled, breathless Andrew appears. "Oh thank God, Lucy. I thought you left."

"Where would I go?"

Andrew shakes his head. "I don't know. I don't know. I wasn't thinking."

"You won't get any argument from me there."

"Look, can we go somewhere and talk?"

"Sure. How about backstage where no one would think to look for us?"

I tap my nose like Stacie did and see the sting on Andrew's face. I pity my best friend. He doesn't yet know how badly he screwed up. Doesn't know how everything is about to change. Oh sure, we'll go somewhere and talk, but he's not going to like what I'm about to say.

·•◉•·

Andrew tries to take my hand as we step into the hallway, but I pull away.

"Luce. Please don't be that way. Nothing happened."

"Why would you put yourself in the position, literally, of making me and Stacie *think* that something might?"

Andrew is confused. "I don't get you."

"Did you ask me to prom hoping I'd sit on some other guy's lap?"

"No."

"What would you have done if I had?"

"But Stacie sat on my lap. What was I supposed to do? Tell her she wasn't allowed? That my girlfriend wouldn't like it? I didn't want to be a jerk."

"And yet, you are."

"I'm sorry, Lucy. So, so sorry. Just tell me what you want me to do and I'll do it."

"It's too late. I didn't want you to leave me tonight to party with Stacie, but you did."

"It'll never happen again, I swear."

Andrew looks so scared. It makes my heart hurt. "Why is it so hard to be mad at you?"

"So don't be. Let's start over. Come on, let's go back inside."

At that moment, I want so badly to follow Andrew back into the junior prom and dance to cheesy mixes like nothing ever happened. We can go to Rafferty's afterward. I'll text Mom like Liam said and ask her to stay out past curfew, then we'll all hit the diner at three in the morning before the limo takes us home.

I want all that. Just like I want to believe that Andrew and

I are meant to be and I'm not about to lose the entire Clark family, and that he doesn't have feelings for Stacie and I don't have feelings for Connor. But I can't because it would be a lie and that would be bad for both of us. I know what I have to do, and it's not out of spite or anger or jealousy.

"I think we should break up." I launch the hard words into the air, then give them time to settle between us.

Andrew says nothing. He just keeps shaking his head. "What if I don't want to? What if I won't let you?"

I take both his hands in mine and look into his eyes, which, like mine, are glassy with tears. "Maybe this is what you want too," I say. "It'll give you a chance to date other people. People like Stacie."

I don't say it to be mean, but anger clouds Andrew's eyes and his expression gets hard. "I told you nothing happened!"

Andrew's voice echoes in the empty hallway and I flinch. I've never heard him get this loud. I wait for his breathing to slow before saying anything more. "I know. I get it. But be honest with yourself. Maybe you wanted something to happen."

"So this is it? You're breaking up with me, and I'm just supposed to walk back into prom with you, pretend nothing happened, and have a good time?"

Now I'm the one getting angry again. "I didn't start this, Andrew. You did. You know what? I don't care what you do because I'm leaving."

"What? You can't leave. How will you get home?"

"I'll ask the limo driver to take me."

"What if he's not out there? What if he says no?"

"Then I'll call my dad, Andrew. Don't worry about it. You're free. Ask another pretty girl to sit in your lap. Go sit in someone else's. I. Don't. Care."

Andrew paces in front of me, running his fingers through his hair. "Tell you what. Just give me tonight, please? And if you still want to break up with me tomorrow, fine. I won't argue. I screwed up, and I'll accept the consequences. But please, Luce, just wait. Wait until tomorrow."

I don't know what to do. This is so hard. I don't want to hurt Andrew, but I don't want to keep hurting each other, doing things that will make it impossible to stay friends. I love Andrew. I have since we were three. Tears trickle down my cheeks.

"I need to fix my makeup," I say.

Andrew wipes a tear from my chin before it hits my dress. "Go ahead. I'll wait here." My throat constricts as he kisses the top of my head because I know it's probably the last time. Why doesn't he get it? If I thought for a second that Andrew was so head-over-heels in love with me that he wouldn't even look at another girl, let alone let her park her rear on his lap, I would follow him back inside right now. I would hold on tight and wait to fall deeply in love with him because he's a great guy and he deserves it. But when I saw Andrew with Stacie, it was like the lights went on and the magic was ruined.

"Go on without me. I'll be okay."

"Sure?"

"I'm sure."

I walk toward the bathroom and wave to him as he opens the cafetorium door and dance music explodes into the quiet hallway. I smile, but inside my heart collapses. The door slams shut, and I take out my phone. My hands shake as I text: Andrew and I just broke up. Can you come and get me? I head down the empty hallway to find an exit.

The base beat fades, the farther I get, and the *swish, swish, swish* of my dress grows louder, filling me with a strange foreboding and loneliness. I'm walking away from more than just some silly prom. I cannot remember a time when there was a Lucy without an Andrew. All I've ever known is down the long hall behind me. Without my friends and brother, I'm untethered, scared, but excited too.

Chapter 15

"Don't be fooled by their smiley mouths or impressive water acrobatics. During mating season, male dolphins are aggressive and manipulative, often forming gangs to spirit away a female and monopolize her attention. Dolphins are highly sexual creatures and by no means monogamous. They are also one of the few creatures to copulate for reasons other than reproduction."

From "What's Love Got to Do with It? The Dating and Mating Habits of North American Sea Life." A junior thesis by Lucy Giordano.

I didn't lie to Andrew. That's what I tell myself as I make my way through the school's visual and performing arts wing. I never said I was going back inside with him. And yet uncertainty and a restless energy rise in me, as they usually do on those rare occasions when I act on impulse and let emotions, not reason, dictate my actions. At times like this, I normally run to Andrew, not away from him. He's the one who's always helped me sort these things out.

Like last October. After my morning with Connor, I didn't go straight home. It was already past the two-hour time limit my dad had given me, but I didn't care. I jumped on my bike and pedaled at lightning speed down Ocean Avenue. The thunderous ocean pounded the surf, and it had begun to rain. There were no cars, no people, no sounds, except for the hollow rush of wind.

I should have been scared, but every nerve ending in my body still felt alive and awakened by Connor's touch; his voice filled my ears. "You're beautiful," he'd said when we stepped onto the porch. "I don't want to say good-bye." I couldn't stop smiling. I had to tell someone.

By the time I reached Andrew's house, I was shaking from both the cold rain and the rush of emotion. There were sandbags on the porch and around the basement's perimeter. The house looked empty, but I parked my bike and walked up the front steps to ring the bell. No one answered, and I was relieved. I had already begun to doubt it was a good idea. I could picture Kiki and Meghan, bug-eyed and breathless, waiting for me to tell them about my morning with Connor, but standing on the Clarks' front steps that day, I couldn't muster that same image of Andrew's reaction. And I knew that if our roles were reversed, I'd feel the same way.

Though neither of us was the type to divulge intimate details, I was always fairly certain I wouldn't want to hear that Andrew had hooked up with another girl. We were best friends and each other's go-to person, but the potential to be more always simmered below the surface. Sharing my Connor news with Andrew that day, or any day after, would have forever changed the special dynamic of our guy-girl friendship.

Tonight we've both said and done things that have blown that all to bits anyway. We were each other's everything, and now, as I push open the heavy exit door and let the warm June air rush in on me, I fear we're about to become nothing at all.

I step out into the twilight and look around to make sure no chaperones are nearby. Not seeing anyone, I walk around to the front of the building. Connor's truck is parked by the curb in the bus drop-off lane. I glance back at the school one more time with equal parts of relief and regret. What have I done? More importantly, what am I going to do?

As I approach Connor, he pops out of the driver's seat, hustles around the car, and opens the door for me. It's like he's my getaway driver.

"Thanks for coming," I say.

"Of course." Connor looks concerned but doesn't ask any questions as he helps me into his truck.

"Maybe I should go back inside," I say when he slides into the driver's seat.

He hesitates before putting his truck in drive. "Is that what you want? I'll walk you in."

I don't know what I want, but clearly it's not for everyone to see Connor walking me into the junior prom. "No. That's okay. I should just go home and not waste any more of your time."

"Seeing you is never a waste of time," he says without looking at me.

"I'm so sorry I dragged you away from Bryn and your friends."

"They're mostly her friends, and it's fine. I told her you broke up with Andrew and needed a ride home. She even offered to come along."

Bryn's reaction surprises me, as does the fact that Connor actually got Andrew's name right this time. But it's nice to hear that Connor told his girlfriend the truth. "Where is she?"

"Her friend Brittany has a place in Toms River. She's having a party. I told her to go on ahead and I'd meet her there."

"Oh."

"You can come too."

I look down at what I'm wearing with an ironic laugh. "I'm a tad overdressed."

"But beautiful."

"Stop."

"It's true."

"It's really not. But thank you." I'm not fishing for compliments. I've had my Cinderella moment, but with all the crying I've done tonight, it's pretty much pumpkin time.

"You can change when you get to your house. I don't mind waiting."

My chest tightens at the thought of going home. We're approaching the bridge, and from there it will be about seven minutes—I know from riding the bus. "Oh God, what am I going to tell my parents?"

"The same thing you told me."

"But how do I explain how I got home? Or why you drove me."

"Tell them I was passing by?"

I groan and put my head in my hands. "I should have thought this through. I'm not good at being daring or spontaneous. I'm methodical. Practical. I don't take chances."

"I'm not so sure about that," Connor says.

I panic, thinking he's going to bring up that day, but he laughs. "I remember watching you and Liam learn to surf. I was dying to learn how myself, but I was still tooling around on a boogie board at that point. You guys must have been... I don't know..."

"Eight," I say, smiling at the memory of the first surfboards Liam and I had. They were Liquid Shredders, with a softer core for beginners, and my parents probably spent more on them than they could afford. Mine was purple with a yellow sunburst design, and Liam's was sort of rust colored. "We got those boards for our eighth birthday."

"I was so jealous. And more than a little fascinated. I watched you guys practicing on the beach. Then wading into the water. You were fearless."

I point to myself, shocked that he even remembers an eight-year-old version of me. "Fearless? Me? You must be remembering Liam. Like I said, risk adverse."

"No, it was definitely you. He was good, but you were better. I remember because I always felt competitive with Liam. Not that he ever knew."

"Don't be too sure," I mumble.

"Liam was more tentative, so I felt kind of smug, thinking I could be better. But you? It took you no more than two tries before you stood up on that board."

I can't believe he's remembering these details. "Are you sure?"

"Positive. I was in awe."

"I always thought Liam was the first to stand up on the board." He was the first to do just about everything else: ride a bike, date, be born.

"No, it was you. You should have seen how determined you were. You were fierce. I developed a serious crush on you that day."

"No, you didn't!"

"I did."

All along, I'd thought it had been me watching him, not the other way around. "You hid it well."

"For years," he says.

My cheeks are on fire, and Connor can't look at me. I thought he was immune to embarrassment. "Why?" I ask. "Why didn't you say something?"

"Because somehow I thought if I ever made a move, your brother would kick my ass."

I laugh. "Who thinks about making a move when they're eight?"

"I was *nine*. And to answer your question: me. I thought about making a move when I was nine. But I thought your brother would get in the way."

"Good instincts. We know that hasn't changed, but something must have."

"You." His eyes dart my way, then back to the road.

"Me?"

He hesitates, and I can tell he's thinking. "You always seemed out of reach. Like you were constantly moving away from me. I'd show up on the beach, and you'd be leaving with your friends. I'd go for a run on the boardwalk, and you'd blow by me on your bike. I'd ask you to go crabbing, and you'd say you'd just been with Andrew. But then last summer—"

"I changed direction?"

Connor nods. "Or at least stopped moving."

Kiki always says my attempts to play it cool around boys come off as *snobbish*. (Keeks's word, not mine.) It's true, I was trying to hide my feelings for Connor—from everyone—but it's possible I went too far the other way. For the longest time, that door stayed locked. But then last July, after he saved Scuttle on the beach, something shifted. I wanted to see what would happen if I let him in.

I turn and smile at him. "I did spend a lot of time on that swing last summer."

The corner of Connor's mouth turns up. "I kind of hoped I had something to do with that." Then he looks over at me and I get the urge to turn the air-conditioning up.

What are we doing? What's the point? It's nice to know that as we sat there together, swaying side by side, we *were* growing closer. I didn't imagine it. But where did that get us? It took two more months and a freak storm to finally bring us together for a few sweet hours, and then *kapow!* We changed directions again. It's time to stop the chain reaction and return to life as a free-floating atom.

"How did you and Bryn meet anyway?" I blurt out, throwing cold water on the direction this conversation is taking. "Sorry. That must've seemed random since you're not inside my head and all."

Connor looks confused. "Uh, okay. Random is fine. I can do random."

I hold up my hand. "You don't have to tell me if you don't want to. I shouldn't be so nosy."

"You're not nosy, and there's not much to tell. I've known Bryn since kindergarten. Well, kindergarten, take one. Remember I was—"

"Redshirted."

"Right. So I've known her a long time." Connor glances over at me. "Sure you want to hear this?"

"Sure. Why not?" *Why not?* Maybe because the thought of Connor being with another girl makes me physically sick?

Connor looks dubious but continues. "So right before winter break, Bryn's longtime boyfriend broke up with her. They'd be going out since freshman year. She was devastated."

"That's a long time."

Connor nods. "She asked me to go to some New Year's party. I didn't feel like going out, but she seemed like she needed someone to talk to and I…I don't know. I guess we were both going through something. It helped. Having someone who understood."

I understood. Better than Bryn, better than anyone. I remember New Year's Eve too. It has never been one of my favorite holidays, but this year, with all of us at Gram's and me still hurting over the phone call from Connor that never happened... I turn my head away. Connor reaches over and brushes my arm, then quickly pulls away.

"Hey, I didn't mean to upset you. I shouldn't have told you."

I nod. "I asked." I still can't look at him. I'm not sure why. What did I expect? One morning with me and he'd never date again? Maybe it's for the best we never amounted to anything. I should have followed my instincts. I always knew a guy like Connor was never meant to be with a girl like me. Then again, most people would say a guy like Andrew was perfect for a girl like me, and look how that turned out. All signs point to me staying single.

I keep my eyes fixed out the window. We're passing the newly rebuilt fishing pier.

"Almost home," I mumble. Then I begin wrapping and unwrapping my hand like a mummy with the strap from my purse. *What now? What do I do when I get home?* Connor picks up on my vibe.

"My parents aren't down this weekend. You can hang out at my house until we get back."

Wait at his house for him to come home with Bryn? No thanks. Screaming parents sound preferable. "I don't know. That would seem kind of weird."

"Why? Because you'd be tempted to snoop around in my underwear drawer or something?"

"Science is all about investigation," I joke. "Wait. You have an underwear drawer?"

"Everyone has an underwear drawer."

"I don't."

Connor's shocked. "How could you not? Where do you keep your underwear?"

"In my pajama drawer," I say.

"Maybe you're keeping your pajamas in your underwear drawer. Did you ever think of that?"

"No. I can honestly say I have never thought of that. My mind is usually consumed with things like, 'Is it my day to clean the clams?' or 'I wonder how I did on that chemistry midterm.' 'The thesis is fifty percent of my grade,' and, oh, my favorite, 'How the heck am I going to tell my parents I broke up with Andrew and left the junior prom with Connor Malloy?'"

I trail off as we turn onto our block and I spy my parents standing under the streetlight in front of our house talking to Mary Colandra, the real estate agent who handles our cottage rental. What is she doing here? And what is that she's holding? I slink down in my seat, out of sight.

"Keep driving!"

"What's wrong?" Connor asks.

"My parents. Do you see them? What are they doing?"

Connor doesn't answer. He drives to the end of the block, makes a right turn onto Ocean Avenue, and pulls over.

"Connor, could you see what they were doing?"

"What are *you* doing?"

"Hiding."

"I get that. Why?"

I sit back up in my seat. "Did you see my parents? Did they see you? I need to know."

"It's dark. I couldn't tell exactly, but it looked like that woman was handing your dad a sign."

This doesn't make sense. I thought Mom had this under control. "What kind of sign? For sale? For rent?"

"I dunno. It looked like a lawn sign. School board election, maybe? For the contractor who worked on your house?"

I shake my head. "No. That woman—the one standing there with them? She rents out our cottage for us, or used to before it got destroyed. I knew this might be coming, but I thought my mom could stop it."

"Stop what?" Connor asks.

"Stop us from *leaving*. The rental money from the cottage pays the taxes on the main house. Without it, we might have to rent our own house for the summer or, worse, sell it. I can't believe this. Could this night get any worse?"

He waves his hands in front of my face and laughs. "You do know I'm sitting here. Right?"

I'm about to apologize when I feel my phone rattle in my bag. Dammit! The Italian half of me should have known better than to tempt fate by saying that out loud. I unlock the screen. Three texts. I wince as I read them. WTF? Where r u? Kiki. Call us.

Let us know you're all right. Meghan. The last one makes me want to cry again. What happened to one more night? Andrew.

I turn off my phone. I can't think straight right now.

"My friends. And Andrew. He wanted me to stay. To wait until tomorrow to decide if we're really over."

"Are you? Really over?"

My chest tightens. I don't want to answer and Connor doesn't press me. Instead, he brushes his knuckles against my arm. "What can I do?"

"You've already done enough. You need to get back to Bryn, and I need to talk to my parents. About more than just prom and Andrew, it seems."

Connor takes out his phone and starts texting. "I'll tell Bryn I'm going to be later than expected."

"Why?"

"Because you're upset and not ready to go home. Trust me, it'll be better if I show up at the party later anyway. Once Bryn gets a few Jell-O shots in her, she won't care where I've been and what time I got there."

"You don't have to do this."

"I know. I want to."

He puts his phone down and looks at me. "There. I'm yours for the next few hours. What do you want to do?"

I turn to face him. I haven't really looked at him since I got in the car. He's got a five-o'clock stubble going on that makes his eyes look even bluer. I consider his questions. There's so much I'd want to do with Connor, if he really were mine. But this is a small town and dressed like I am, there aren't too many places I can go where I wouldn't be seen.

What were the names of his parents' friends? The ones who own my favorite house. Bob and Jane? I wonder if they're here this weekend. What am I thinking? Technically, Andrew and I are together until tomorrow, and more than technically, Connor is Bryn's boyfriend, so that doesn't leave many options.

"How about we just take a ride?"

"Sure. Where to?"

"Up the coast. We can decide on the way."

Connor smiles at this idea. "Let's go," he says and puts the car in drive.

Chapter 16

"Blue crabs can be clingy and opportunistic. During mating season, the male waits until the female is in her soft-shell stage when her defenses are, quite literally, down. Then he attaches himself to her until fertilization and the regrowth of her shell are complete."

From "What's Love Got to Do with It? The Dating and Mating Habits of North American Sea Life." A junior thesis by Lucy Giordano.

Connor and I drive north toward Asbury Park with music playing and the windows down. I steal glimpses into people's homes lit from within. Snippets from strangers' lives. A baseball game on a giant flat-screen TV, a grandfather clock next to an oval mirror, a family sitting down to a late dinner.

We pass through the area that became known as ground zero after the storm, the spot where the bridge was washed out and the storm surge caused the ocean waters to meet the bay. Eight months later, houses still lie on their sides or collapsed in unrecognizable heaps.

"Wow," Connor says. "It looks like the hurricane happened yesterday."

"You should have seen it eight months ago."

Alongside the road, debris piles wait to be removed by the ever-present bulldozers and dump trucks, and there's an entire stretch where the beachfront can now be seen from the road because, sadly, there's nothing left in between. For my entire life, that view was obstructed by multimillion-dollar estates with lush landscaping and security gates.

I've always known the ocean was powerful. That it was a force I had to respect, but it's still difficult for me to picture the enormity of the ocean swells that swept ten-bedroom homes off hundred-year-old foundations and ripped them out to sea.

"It looks like a tornado came through here," Connor says.

"Yeah, it does. More than one."

We arrive in Asbury Park, and I take him past the legendary Stone Pony and Convention Hall, two New Jersey landmarks made famous by Bruce Springsteen and hallowed ground for countless musicians and bands. The Pony, which luckily only suffered minor damages during the storm, was one of the first clubs to host Superstorm Sandy relief concerts, and the front of Convention Hall is where President Obama stood and pledged the government's support after touring the devastation with the governor. I went there with my family to hear him speak.

"Let's get out and walk around," Connor suggests.

But I'm too self-conscious about my prom dress. I'm also worried about him getting back to Bryn and me facing my parents, Liam, my friends, and Andrew. Ugh. I can't put it off much longer.

"Next time," I say. "We'll walk out onto the pier, then get our palms read by Madam Marie. She's a fortune-teller made famous after Bruce mentioned her in a song."

"Oh, yeah? Which one?"

"Fourth of July, Asbury Park."

"How do you even know that?" Connor asks.

"Liam."

"So let's do it now. I want to find out what that famous Madame Marie has to say about my future."

I shake my head. "I'm afraid I'm giving off nothing but negative energy tonight."

"Come on. I'm not taking no for an answer. One quick palm reading and we'll head straight back." Connor raises his hand like he's making the Boy Scout promise. "Swear."

How can I say no? He left his girlfriend on prom weekend to come rescue my weepy butt.

"Okay. But you're going first."

"What happened to fierce Lucy?"

I shrug and give him a half smile. "When I find her, I'll let you know."

Madame Marie's cement shack sits near Convention Hall and the pier. It's painted deep blue and decorated with mystical symbols, one of which is a giant eye. It's close to ten o'clock and the neon signs—"Readings" and "Advisor"—cast a red glow on this deserted stretch of boardwalk. Like ours, the boards have been replaced.

Bells on the door announce our arrival. "I'm surprised she's still open," I whisper to Connor.

"It's like she was waiting for us." Connor attempts to sound mystical.

A woman steps out from behind a velvet curtain. She's wearing skinny jeans, high boots, and a long, blousy top. She's about sixty and too old for her youthful getup, but other than that, she looks relatively normal. No heavy eyeliner, turban, or wizard's robe.

"Can I help you?"

"We're here for a reading," Connor says.

"Together or separate?" she asks.

"Separate," I practically shout before Connor can answer. "He'd like to go first."

"Okay... Step this way, uh—"

"Connor."

"Connor. Nice Irish name. I'm Madame Ava."

"Not Marie?"

"Not Marie."

She holds back the curtain for Connor, who turns and wiggles his eyebrows at me before stepping inside.

As I wait, the smell of incense makes me slightly queasy. I realize I hardly ate anything at the prom. I look around the small waiting room. On the wall is a framed obituary for Madame Marie Costella. She died in 2008 when she was in her nineties.

Wow, she had been telling fortunes on the boardwalk since the 1930s. Apparently she told Bruce he was going to be a big star. Bruce claims she said that to all the rockers.

After exhausting all the available reading material, I walk over to the glass door and stare out at the blackened waves. What's taking him so long? Finally, Connor pops out from behind the curtain and calls, "Next!"

"What'd she say?" I ask as I pass him on the way in.

"Wouldn't you like to know?"

"Funny," I say and give him a light punch on the arm. I step inside the small, dark room with a plain, circular table and two velvet-backed chairs. "I'm Lucia. Lucy."

"Nice to meet you, Lucy." She motions to the red velvet chair. "Sit, please. Are you right-handed or left-handed?"

"Left. Does it make a difference?"

"Your dominant hand will tell me what's going on now. The passive hand indicates inherited characteristics."

"Ah."

"Now place both hands on the table, palms facing up."

I do as she says and feel her eyes giving me the once-over. "Prom or wedding?" she asks.

"Prom."

"I get the feeling Connor wasn't your date."

"Is that a psychic feeling or just a regular one?" I'm guessing the latter since Connor looks underdressed for prom.

"Sweetheart, I'm a palm reader, not a psychic. And you don't need either to tell you he may be the right guy, but this is the wrong time." And then she takes my left hand in hers and begins to examine the lines etched into my skin that will tell her my destiny.

•• ◉ ••

As soon as we're back in the car, Connor starts bugging me about Madame Ava's reading.

"Come on. Tell me," he pleads.

"You first."

"Fine. So, she compared both palms."

"The dominant and passive," I say.

"Correct. She said she can tell I want to change."

"For the better?"

His whole body sighs. "Luce."

"I'm sorry. Go on."

"Well, she said my love line had short lines crossing it, indicating I have a hard time with fidelity," Connor says.

"Hmm. Maybe she's the real deal."

"Hey, when it comes to girls, I admit I have ADD, but I've never been dishonest with the girls I've dated. I never led them to believe I wanted a relationship."

"Until Bryn?" Funny how I'd put her out of my head until just now. "She's your first real relationship?"

His jaw tightens and he scrunches his eyebrows. "Technically, I guess. But she wasn't the first girl I wanted a relationship with."

"Connor—"

148

His phone vibrates, and I'm relieved I don't have to go on. I wasn't exactly sure what to say. Connor glances at the screen, then turns it off. I don't ask. Then he turns to me and flashes that Connor smile no girl can resist. I can tell it's forced, that he's probably in trouble with Bryn right now, but I appreciate that he's trying to keep things upbeat.

"Come on, your turn," he says. "Tell me what Madame Ava said about you."

I turn sideways in my seat, which isn't easy in my gown, and try to match his enthusiasm. "Okay, so. She said I have a strong, straight fate line."

"Meaning?"

"I'm career-minded and focused."

"Anyone who knows you for more than five minutes could have told you that."

"Ah, but she *doesn't* know me. Don't tell me you're doubting the great Madame Ava's gift? This was your idea, remember? You're the one who wanted to experience palmistry."

"I wanted to experience palmistry with *you*. We have good palmistry together, don't you think?"

"I think so, but it's hard to be sure," I say.

"Why's that?"

"I have nothing to compare it to. I've never done palmistry with anyone but you." I wait for his reaction. A comeback laced with innuendo. But he says nothing.

When we stop at a red light, he takes my hand and unfolds my fingers. With his index finger, he traces my open palm, sending shivers everywhere. I fight to keep my eyes open and not get lost in this moment. "What did she say about your love line?" he asks.

I try to steady my breathing, but I'm hyperaware of my rapidly rising and falling chest. Finally, the light turns green and I slip my hand out of his. "That I should stay away from boys who can't keep their hands to themselves and their eyes on the road."

He looks impatient all of a sudden. "For real, Luce. What'd she say?"

I let out a dramatic sigh. "That I'm guarded. I don't fall in love easily." That's only half true.

"That's it, nothing else?" It's like he senses I'm holding back.

"That's it," I say, leaving out the part where, right before I left, Madame Ava pressed both my hands together and said: *You've gotten off course, but you'll find your way back to him.*

"How?" I asked.

I was curious to hear what she had to say, even if it turned out to be a pile of horse poop. She looked at me with small, laser-focused gray eyes that in that instant made me want to believe she had the answer I've been looking for.

"By going back to the beginning and starting again," she said.

I stared at her. Was she trying not to smile? "Thank you," I said and pushed my chair away from the table. Madame Ava stood too. "Of course," she said.

I began to walk away, and as I placed my hand on the curtain, she said: "I noticed you didn't ask 'who.'"

"What?" I asked.

She blew out the candle on her table, then looked at me. "When I said you'll find your way back to him, you never asked who."

• ● •

It's just after midnight when Connor turns onto our block.

"All the lights are on downstairs. That can't be good."

Connor parks the car by the curb, across the street from our houses. "Do you want me to walk you in?"

"Thanks, but no. It'll make it worse."

"Things will get better. Madame Ava told me so," Connor declares.

"Do you believe everything Madame Ava said?"

"Don't you?"

He turns and stares without saying anything. He's making me nervous.

"What?" I ask.

"Nothing. I had fun tonight."

"Me too." I did, even though it began with drama and was likely to end with more. The few hours I had alone with Connor felt almost like a first date.

"See? I told you tonight would get better." He leans closer, as if he can hear what I'm thinking. Against my better judgment—and my own free will, it seems—I lean toward him. He slips his hand under my hair, and I tilt my head. Our lips are close to touching when I give myself a hard mental slap: "Crap!"

He jumps and looks over his shoulder, thinking there's someone standing next to the car. "What's wrong?"

Connor belongs to someone else. Kissing him would make me no better than Stacie. I'm angry with myself for letting things get that far again. *Must my brain take a vacation whenever I get close to Connor?*

"I gotta go! Tell Bryn I said 'thank you' for letting me borrow you."

"I will," Connor says. He looks disappointed, but I know I'm doing the right thing. We both are. He gives my hand a quick squeeze. "Good night, Lucy Goosey."

"It was a good night," I say. "Thanks to you."

Then I open the door and hustle across the street. The porch light clicks on by the time my foot hits the first step. Clearly, I was being watched.

"Where have you been?" Mom pounces as soon as I walk into the living room. "And don't bother to tell me prom, because Meghan already called. I know you left early."

"Meghan called *you*?"

"Yes. At least someone had the sense to. She was worried. She said you and Andrew had a big fight and that you wanted to leave early. Do you have any idea how worried we've been? Your father was going to call the police."

I wonder if she'll ask Liam why he didn't call to check up on me. If I know my brother, he didn't want to do anything to implicate himself in the situation. If he threw me under the bus, I'd drag him under the wheels with me.

"I didn't mean to make everyone worry. I'm so sorry, Mom, really. It's just…me and Andrew? We broke up."

Mom's face softens. "I'm sorry, honey. But why didn't you call us? You know we're always here for you."

"Because I wanted to leave and I didn't want you or Dad to stop me. Prom cost you guys a lot of money. My leaving early was kind of a waste."

"This isn't about the money, Lucy. It's about you making wise choices and being safe."

I'm dying to tell her all about the wise choice my brother made tonight.

"Who drove you home? Was that Connor?" She knows it was. I'm afraid to answer, but I do. "Yes."

Mom crosses her arms. "So you left the prom with another boy?" She knows I did, though her face screams: *Oh no, you didn't!*

"We're just friends."

"Since when?"

"I don't know, since always. He has lived next door all my life. Why are you so surprised?"

"The Clarks are our friends. They *live* here. The Malloys are part-timers."

"So? Maybe they're really nice people. You and Dad never got to know them."

"We know them." Mom sounds defensive.

"Have you ever had a real conversation with Connor's mom? Maybe you've got a lot in common. You should—"

Mom cuts me off. "Don't tell me what I should be doing. This isn't about me being friends with Mrs. Malloy. This is about you leaving prom with her son and not telling us. What have you been doing for the past three hours while I've been here going out of my mind?"

"Riding around."

"Riding around? With Connor? On prom night. We didn't raise you to be like that, Lucy."

"To be like what? The kind of girl who feels hurt and humiliated when she discovers her boyfriend sharing a flask with another girl? Did I mention that girl was sitting on his lap? Are you going to tell me I overreacted, just like Liam did?"

I shouldn't have let the alcohol thing slip, but I'm hurt and pissed. Maybe calling Connor for a ride wasn't the smartest thing I've ever done, but always doing the right thing is starting to get on my nerves.

Mom's shaking her head. "I'm very disappointed in Andrew. But you still should have called *us*, not Connor, or at least come straight home."

"I *did* come straight home. But I didn't want to interrupt your secret meeting with Mary Colandra."

"How did you—"

"I saw Mary, Mom. And her stupid sign. Where is it anyway?"

I glance around the living room but don't see it lying around anywhere.

"We were going to tell you in the morning. We wanted to meet with Mary about renting or selling the house privately. While you and Liam were out."

"Yeah, I got that part. So now we're *selling* the house?"

"Not if we can rent the house for most of the summer."

"You said you wouldn't let this happen."

"I don't like it any more than you do. I've lived in this house all my life. But the rental money will cover our taxes and help with constructing a new rental cottage. Still, your father wants to keep our options open."

"I don't want to leave. Even if it is just for the summer."

"Someday you'll find out there's a difference between what you want to happen and what *needs* to happen."

Someday?

I wanted one boy. I needed the other. And I both want *and* need this house. What happens now?

Chapter 17

"Love hurts. Having a thick skin can be very useful for enduring the ups and downs of relationships. Female blue sharks should know. Their skin is three times thicker than males', a trait critical for a female to survive bites from her mate during copulation."

From "What's Love Got to Do with It? The Dating and Mating Habits of North American Sea Life." A junior thesis by Lucy Giordano.

I spent the forty-eight hours after prom holed up in my room and driving myself insane listening to the various comings and goings of those who would not speak to me (Liam and my friends), those I could not be seen speaking to (Connor), and those to whom I had nothing to say (my parents).

There was the slamming of doors. The jangling of keys. The crunch of footsteps on stones. The smell of coffee brewing. The rise and fall of murmuring voices. The sun rising and setting against my closed window shade without me ever venturing outside. I timed my movements with the sound of absolute silence, choosing to eat in my room. I barely changed out of my pajamas. It felt like I had the flu.

Throughout the weekend, Connor was in regular contact. Or tried to be. I wanted to be alone and didn't answer his every text or call. He wanted to see me before he left for home, but I told him it wasn't a good idea. By Sunday night, I *looked* like I had the flu. More importantly, he had a girlfriend, and I had several relationships that needed repairing.

I hadn't heard from any of my friends except Kiki who texted me on Saturday morning, after prom. Thanks for ruining my night. She was with my brother and he didn't get home until 5:00 a.m. (What happened to that curfew, Mom?), so how awful could it have been? I thought at the very least Andrew would have called to apologize or argue some more. Why would he let us go without a fight?

I found out this morning at school.

"Andrew thinks you cheated on him with Connor," Meghan says while I'm at my locker getting ready to begin the last full week of school.

"Hello to you too." I slam my locker shut and face her. I'm kind of pissed at her for calling my mom, though I know I have no right to be. I wasn't answering my texts, and I know she did it because she cares. Just like I know she's standing here right now for the same reason.

"Look, Luce, I don't want to judge, and you don't owe me an answer, but you should talk to Andrew."

"I would have if he called this weekend."

"The phone works both ways."

"How did he become the victim here? He's the one who got the lap dance."

"You left prom with another guy."

"Who told you?"

"Who do you think? Liam. I gather it wasn't exactly a secret at your house."

"Connor gave me a *ride*. Nothing happened." Technically, it's true, but I know in my heart it's more complicated than that.

The look on Meghan's face tells me she does too. "Look, I'm out of here at the end of fourth period. I'm leaving for Cali tomorrow and I gotta pack. But if you need to talk, just let me know."

Meghan's family visits her mom's sister on the west coast every June. Lucky Meghan—she's getting out of school four days early. They bought their tickets before the school year got extended due to the storm.

"Thank you."

"For the record, what Andrew did wasn't cool, but what you did wasn't too cool either. It would help if we knew your side of the story."

I nod my head. "Understood." The question is: how much of my side of the story do I want to tell? "Meghan?"

"Yeah?" She looks excited, like I'm about to spill right now and tell her everything in the two minutes we've got left before homeroom. I hate to disappoint my only ally.

"Thanks again."

She puts a hand on my shoulder. "Of course."

"Have a great trip."

I wish I were going with her.

"Don't worry. It'll all work out."

I also wish I could believe her.

At lunch, I sit by myself, with only my stupid thirty-page thesis to keep me company. I can't believe I got a B minus! The competition to be valedictorian next year is tight, and this is not going to help my average. I never got a B, let alone a B minus. The note scrawled in red across the front says the writing was solid and my research was impressive, but ultimately I did not support my conclusion that animal dating and mating rituals are more beneficial to species' survival than those in the human world. *What?* How many more examples did I need? My thesis was ten pages longer than it needed to be.

I stuff my paper into my tote bag, then throw out my uneaten lunch. What does Ms. Stouffer know? I should've played it safe and written about stupid Romeo and Juliet. I know I'm right. Sex without love and solely for the purpose of procreation is less messy, emotionally painful, and dangerous than giving too much to a boy who can't be trusted or one who can never be yours.

My week only gets worse from there. On Tuesday, I find out I did not get the internship on Sedge Island. Something about more people competing for fewer slots. This is an even bigger blow than the lousy grade on my thesis. It affects my whole future.

Marine mammalogy is my dream, but it's a highly competitive field. I need as much hands-on experience as possible before I apply to colleges in the fall. It's practically too late to find another marine science internship, and besides, Sedge

Island was perfect because I could bike there or hitch a ride from my dad. I won't have a driver's license for at least a few more weeks, and even if I pass my road test, I don't have a car.

On Wednesday, my parents make an announcement at dinner. "Mary found us some renters," Mom says. She looks nervous.

"We're moving out in August," Dad adds.

"Well, that's just freaking great," Liam says. Then in true Liam fashion, he stands up, slams his chair into the table, and walks out the back door. Leaving me to wonder how he always gets away with being the difficult twin, while I have one lapse in judgment at the stinkin' junior prom and it's like the whole universe is against me.

Somehow I've made it to Friday, the last day of school, and I'm riding the bus home alone because I didn't want to wait for my parents to clean their desks and Kiki, Liam, and Andrew still aren't talking to me. Or maybe I'm not talking to them. All I know is, the longer people go without reaching out to each other, the harder it gets to make an attempt.

And Connor, who has been very supportive of everything, is eighty miles away and still with Bryn. He says he's going to ask his father's opinion about rebuilding our rental cottage and thinks I need to open the lines of communication with my friends.

"Talk to Kiki," he said when he called last night. "Make things right with her first."

The school bus lurches down Route 37 toward home. Even with all the windows open, it still smells like an old sneaker.

I should be out on the waves with my friends right now. It's a last-day-of-school tradition—surfing, followed by a barbecue at Andrew's. I guess this year Liam will be taking my spot around the Clarks' backyard fire pit. Hope he burns his tongue on a marshmallow.

Had it not been for Hurricane Sandy, I would have said these past seven days have been the absolute worst ever, but I hate feeling sorry for myself and I've also learned to keep such hyperbole in check. I take out my phone to play a word game without friends and instead wind up dialing Connor's number. His last day of school isn't until next week, and he's due back in Seaside by July first to start his volunteer work rebuilding. His phone rings for a while, then goes to voice mail.

I disconnect as the bus rolls to a halt and the kid behind me moans, "Crap. The bridge is going up."

There's nothing we can do but sit and wait. This could take a while. I look out the window. We're stopped right where the state police set up their checkpoint the morning we were finally allowed to temporarily return to our homes after the hurricane. I was riding a school bus that day too, only I wasn't alone. I was with my family and lots of other people I knew from town.

It was ten days after Superstorm Sandy, and we were being shuttled onto the island to see if our homes were still standing and to collect belongings and necessities that got left behind. The island still had no running water, natural gas, or electricity. It wasn't completely safe to stay, and the roads were not yet open to regular traffic. We were all on edge.

"It is what it is," I heard Mr. McCauley say to Dad while we waited to board the bus.

Andrew and his family had arrived later than us and were taking the next shuttle. We hugged for a long time after he spotted me in line. "Call me later and let me know how your day went."

"I will," I said. "Keep an eye out for Kiki and Meghan. They texted that they'd be here, but I haven't seen them anywhere."

Everyone on our bus was silent as we were waved through the checkpoint. It felt like we were entering a war zone. When we reached the bridge's highest point, I looked out over the expansive bay. There wasn't a single boat in sight, only lonely buoys rocking in the waves and a few seagulls gliding along the surface.

"I shouldn't have come," I said to Liam. "I don't want to see how bad the house looks. I don't want to know."

"It's still standing. We saw it."

He was talking about the images of our house on NOAA's website. The National Oceanic and Atmospheric Administration posted "before and after" aerial views of the entire area. As soon as Gram's town house regained power, we were able to log on and see our house's roof, so we knew it was still standing, as were the rest of the houses on our block, including the Malloys'. That morsel of relief felt good, and it crossed my mind that I should text Connor about the website, but we knew the photos couldn't tell us how far the floodwaters had reached before receding.

Still, we were thankful. A mere three miles up the coast, the oceanfront bungalows had been knocked from their foundations, as if an angry arm had swept across a Monopoly board and left the game in ruins.

As we approached the other side of the bridge, we craned our necks and held a collective breath as we got our first glimpse of Pelican Island, the tiny island before ours, which is no more than a quarter mile wide and less than a half mile long. Every house there was within a few blocks of the bay. That day, unbelievably, some of them were *in* the bay. I remember it took my brain a few second to adjust to what I was seeing.

On certain blocks, the waterfront homes were just gone. The streets were clogged with sand and debris—two-by-fours, patio chairs, barbecues, umbrellas, yard toys. Abandoned cars and damaged boats lined the roadsides, and power lines were down. The shattered windows of storm-ravaged houses gaped at us, the shards of glass like broken teeth. It looked like the work of bombs, not bay waters. My stomach tightened and the tears began to fall. When I looked sideways at Liam, he pinched the bridge of his nose and closed his eyes.

"Everything's going to be all right, Luce," he said with his eyes still shut tight. He put his hand out, and I took it, holding on to my brother as the bus rounded the jug handle near the WaveRunner rental place, where the fishing pier had been. Four pilings remained, marking its beginning and end, but every board in between was gone. Boats that had lost their moorings had drifted into the shallow cove. Nothing looked right. It was like some distorted nightmare version of the place where I grew up.

The bus stopped on Central Avenue, our version of Main Street, and the town official who'd ridden there with us stood up and made an announcement. "We'll be making block-by-block stops to leave you off at your homes. Do not leave your property! The area is not safe, and this is no time for sightseeing. The buses will be making frequent runs back and forth across the bridge with the last one leaving at four p.m. I do not want to leave anyone behind."

The bus dropped the four of us off near the Windjammer Motor Inn, which is in the middle of town and close to our house. No one said a word as we practically ran home. In our front yard were two crumpled beach chairs, several garbage cans, a flower pot, and a plastic pumpkin. None of them ours. Dad fumbled with the key before finally getting the front door open. Mom walked in first and immediately began to cry. Dad was next, followed by Liam.

I lingered on the porch, even more afraid of what was waiting for us now that we were here. I stood there for a while, looking at the Malloys' house, ashamed to admit I was relieved theirs was still standing too and hoping I'd see Connor that day. I don't know how long I stood there before Liam came back for me. He put a hand on my shoulder. "Come on, Luce. It's not as bad as you think. We'll walk in together."

My older brother. He could be all right. His austerity gave me strength sometimes.

Inside, the floodwaters had receded, but I could smell that dank odor and see the watermark on the walls and stone fireplace that the bay had left behind. My fish were all dead. Stiff and floating in one corner of the tank. It's not like they're cute and furry and interactive like dogs and cats, but they were mine and I felt awful. Throw pillows and magazines were strewn on the floor, and though you couldn't tell by looking at them, I was sure the TV and the DVD player and all the kitchen appliances were ruined. I've heard burglary victims talk about feeling violated after a break-in. That's how I felt. Violated by the horrific storm.

An hour later, I stepped out onto the porch for some air and Keeks was there holding a cardboard tray with hot chocolates and doughnuts. Her cheeks were red with cold and she was crying.

"From the Red Cross." Her voice cracked as she shrugged her shoulders. "They had Boston cream. Your favorite."

On the school bus on the last day of school, the gate opens and the bus moves forward. But my mind is still back in that other day. Having Kiki show up like that made one of the worst moments better. Connor's right. I have to talk to her.

I arrive at Breakwater Burrito the next day determined to make things right, but my resolve fades fast when I see Kiki. She walks through the back door, her bangs a foreboding red, and I manage a quick "Hey" and a half smile before she storms past me like I'm invisible. After that, I work beside Kiki on the takeout line with my stomach in knots. By midafternoon, the tension between us is palpable.

"Everything okay between you and Karina?" Adela asks when I take my break.

"Not really."

"What happened?" she asks.

"Long story."

"Well, I'll make time if you want to talk about it."

"I'm hoping I can work things out with Keeks and there won't be much to tell. But thank you, Adela. I really appreciate it."

She gives me a big, squishy hug. "Of course. You kids are like family."

I spend the rest of my six-hour shift mulling over what I'm going to say to Kiki the next time I get the chance. When our shift ends, Kiki is packing up her stuff in the kitchen and I know I have to act fast. Before she can get away, I stand between her and the back door.

"Kiki, I'm sorry," I rush to say. She's already sidestepping me. "I know you're mad because I left the prom."

She lets her bag drop off her shoulder and finally makes eye contact with me. "Do you really think that's the only reason I'm mad? You're the stupidest smart person I know."

"Is it because of Connor? Meghan told me what everyone thinks, but nothing happened. I swear. It's just...after I saw Andrew with Stacie and I told him I wanted to break up, all I wanted to do was get out of there."

"Maybe I would have known that if you talked to your friends. Meghan and I didn't even know why you were so upset. We had to hear it from Andrew."

"Oh and I'm sure he made it sound like it was all innocent."

"At least he told us, Luce. That's what friends do. You just left."

"I'm sorry. I panicked and I ran."

"To Connor. Since when did he become the first person you turn to? I thought I was your best friend." Her brow is furrowed and she looks hurt.

"You are."

"Best friends don't keep secrets. I've always told you everything. I *knew* there was something going on between you two when he came in here Memorial Day weekend looking for you."

She's getting louder, which makes me want to talk softer or not at all. "There's nothing going on between us. He has a girlfriend."

"Then why don't you fix things with Andrew? That Stacie girl is just some ho. She doesn't mean anything to him. We could have the perfect summer, you and Andrew, Meghan and Mateo, me and Liam. That's how it was supposed to go."

Wait. What? I knew they had fun at the prom, but I didn't expect my brother to stick around. "You and Liam?"

She scowls. "Yeah. Me and Liam. Don't sound so surprised."

"It's just that I didn't know."

"It sucks when your best friend keeps stuff from you, doesn't it?"

Touché. She's right to be angry. Kiki's openness can be disarming at times, but I admire her ability to share what's inside her. I'm not sure what she sees in Liam. I may have a hard shell, but he's prickly. Like a puffer fish.

Kiki continues. "So you and Connor. Maybe nothing happened after prom, but something happened, am I right?"

I know this is my opening, the path back to my old life with my old friends, but how do I begin to explain to Kiki what happened with Connor at the house on Ocean Avenue? I don't fully understand what led me to act on pure emotion without ever once stopping to consider the consequences. I don't know how to put that day into words, but I do know that this isn't the time or the place for it. Kiki mistakes my silence for a refusal to answer.

"That's what I thought," she snipes. "I thought we were getting somewhere. Guess I was wrong. Tell you what, you know where to find me when you're ready to be honest." Then she pushes past me, banging the door on her way out.

At home, Liam's in the driveway washing Mom's car, which he's hoping to score temporary ownership of next month. Andrew got Liam a job OTB at Rafferty's, or so I heard from my parents. It never would have occurred to me to call dibs on the car, and I didn't care all that much about passing my road test. But not getting the Sedge Island internship changed all that. If

I want more internship options this summer, I need a license and a car.

"Hey," I say as I walk toward him.

"Hey," he says.

I'm surprised he responded. All week, he only spoke to me if our parents were in earshot. I stare at my brother for a few seconds as he suds the tire rims and mocks me with his cool avoidance. He's quite the multitasker. When did the distance between us get so huge? Prom didn't cause this; we've been drifting for years.

As twin babies, we started our lives in some pretty cramped quarters—first in utero, then in the same crib for weeks after we were born. There's a picture of us holding tiny hands in the bassinette when we were only three weeks old. It's one of Mom's screensavers that flashes on the computer when it goes into sleep mode. There are others too—me and Liam digging in the sand…sitting side by side on the kiddie rides…wading into the water with our boards. Beautiful moments frozen in time that only make me sad. I wonder if there's any chance of us getting back there, of becoming more than siblings and actually friends.

Liam looks up from the car's back bumper. "Luce?"

I raise my eyebrows and smile. "Yeah?"

"If you end up with the douche bag, don't expect me to be cool with that."

I turn and walk into the house, not wanting to give him the satisfaction of seeing the hopeful look fall from my face. I don't know when we'll ever be friends again, but obviously it's not today.

Chapter 18

"When it's not breeding season, northern leopard frogs lead solitary lives. They tolerate other frogs but do not need a companion to survive."

From "What's Love Got to Do with It? The Dating and Mating Habits of North American Sea Life." A junior thesis by Lucy Giordano.

It's Sunday morning and I'm at the marina dressed like a giant clam. If I'd known that raising awareness about Reclam Our Waters would involve me looking ridiculous, I might have stayed in bed this morning. My uncomfortable getup is part of a scavenger hunt for kids. Giant faux clam shells containing clues—the educational kind that help kids learn about shore conservation—have been placed all around town.

One clam leads to the next, with the final clue leading back to the marina to me, the keeper of the prize packs donated by local businesses and the radio station. Other volunteers are answering questions about the upweller and handing out pamphlets and car magnets, but I'm the only one dressed like a mollusk. I'm the cheese who stands alone. Only I'm a clam.

"Why do I have to wear the costume?" I whined at the volunteer coordinator, Hank, when I arrived.

"Because I'd make one ugly clam," he said. "Plus, the costume is about your size."

Like there's such a thing as an attractive clam? I'm completely encased in two closed shells. Only my head, hands, and legs stick out. A sharp bay breeze is whipping my hair around, and although I'm longing for a ponytail holder, I wouldn't be able to reach my head anyway.

"A clam on a half shell would have been a lot better, Hank. Don't you think?" I call to him as I mill around and wait for kids to return from the hunt.

"You're a living, thriving creature," Hank says. "Not food."

"Right," I say.

I step onto the grass and let my eyes wander toward the flea market on the green. A jewelry stand catches my eye, and I'm about to waddle in that direction when a voice behind me says: "Did you lose a bet?"

I spin around like a top, nearly losing my balance, and find myself face-to-face with a guy. A very attractive guy, with black curly hair, dark eyes, and long lashes.

"Huh? Oh no, I'm a volunteer with Reclam Our Waters. We're doing a scavenger hunt for kids today."

"I know," he says. "I'm visiting my sister. She brought her five-year-old daughter, and I tagged along to see what it was all about. How'd you get involved with this group anyway?"

"Well, I live here, and I want to be a marine biologist—

specifically a marine mammalogist. Reclam Our Waters sounded like a cool program. And they have a clam college and everything."

"It scares me that you're excited about something called clam college."

"It scares *me* that oysters have all but disappeared from our bay and the clam population is severely diminished."

He nods. "Clams are an indicator species. It *is* alarming that there are so few."

I squint at him. "So you totally get what we're doing."

"I do. The bay needs more oysters and clams. They're natural filters. They eat algae and remove dirt and nitrogen pollution."

I love it when someone talks shellfish to me!

"Exactly. Oysters can filter fifty gallons an hour. More clams and oysters mean cleaner water. We believe that if we can reclam the bay…"

"You can reclaim it."

"I'd high-five you but I can't." I flop my hands to illustrate this point.

He walks around to the side of my shell and offers his hand. We manage an awkward shake. "I'm Chad. I'm majoring in marine conservation at Rutgers."

"Awesome. Our group works in cooperation with Rutgers. You should think about volunteering."

"I just might."

At that moment, a little girl comes charging at me, with two boys on her heels. A mom holding an infant in one of those pouchlike carriers trails behind looking frazzled. The kids are waving their maps and not slowing down. They hit me head-on and nearly knock me over with excitement. Chad catches me by the shell.

"Whoa there, Chloe. Go easy on the clam," Chad says.

"I did it, I did it, Uncle Chad!" shouts the little girl. "I found all the clues!"

"Good for you. Now bring it down a notch, okay?" Chad says. "Stay here with the nice young *woman* while I help your mom with that diaper bag."

"All right then," I say. "Follow me over to the upweller to see some real, live clams and get your prizes."

"Yay, prizes!" Chloe screams and starts waving her map around again. The next thing I know, a wind gust takes it from her hand and blows it toward the curb. Chloe takes off after her map and I take off after her, and for some reason, the two boys get caught up in the moment and take off after me. Chloe's in the middle of the street, with one white-sandaled foot planted on her map, by the time the boys and I reach her.

"Chloe!" I hear behind me.

Chad grabs the girl's hand and retrieves her map all in one swift motion. Chloe's mom and the baby arrive seconds later. We're all standing in the middle of the street—Chloe, the boys, Chad, the mom and baby, and me—when Andrew flies by on his skateboard. He does a double take and my breakfast feels like it wants to make an escape. For a second I think he'll turn around and come back, but after looking over his shoulder one more time, he continues on down the street until he turns into a speck in the distance.

I don't know how long I stand there in the street, staring after him. Chad stays with me, but his sister, Chloe, and the boys have gone to retrieve their prizes. Squeals of laughter erupt from the dock behind me, and I turn. Two little kids run from a snapping crab skittering toward them. In that moment, a deep sadness comes over me. I know even if we get over what happened at the prom, things will never be the same with me and Andrew.

"That was my boyfriend," I blurt out. "We broke up a little more than a week ago, and I haven't seen him since. And then he just passes me in the street on his skateboard? I can't believe he didn't stop."

To Chad's credit, he seems unfazed by my revelation. "Did he see you?"

I nod. "He did a double take."

"Wouldn't you, if you saw him in a clam costume?"

His smile is so warm and inviting that I can't help myself. I start rambling. "I know we're not talking to each other, and it's partly my fault, but I thought he would wave or say 'hey' *something*. You know?"

We start back to the upweller, and by the time I amble over, I've given Chad the "Lucy on speed" version of everything that's happened to me since prom. Beginning with the lap dance, including the ride home from Connor, the B minus on my paper, the renters' August arrival, and ending with how I didn't get the Sedge Island internship. I'm spent, in a good way. I understand now how freeing therapy can be.

"Well, I can't do anything about the rest, but I may be able to help with that last part."

"The internship?"

He nods. "I know about an opportunity that may be better than Sedge Island, especially for someone who wants to go into marine mammalogy."

"Really?"

Chad nods and reaches for his phone. "Do you have an email address?"

"Yeah, why?"

"I know the folks at the marine stranding center down the coast. I interned there the summer after my freshman year at Rutgers. If you give me your email, I'll put you in touch with the right person."

I rattle off my email address and cell number. "Are you serious? You mean I'd get to work with harbor seals and dolphins? I thought they only took college students." My shell is shaking.

"For the internships with direct animal contact, they do only take college students. But they look for volunteers to help with their summer camps for kids. Still, it's a great opportunity and will give you a leg up if you want to apply for an internship next year. You've picked the most competitive branch of marine biology. A gig like this could make a difference. It's a bit of ride from here." He squints. "You are old enough to drive, aren't you?"

"Yes, no. Well, almost. I've got my permit. I'm taking my road test in July."

"Good. A smart girl like you should have no trouble passing."

Shit! A smart girl like me breezed through the written test, but I haven't been behind the wheel in ages. Mom keeps wanting to teach me how to parallel park, but I have no interest. Now it might be too late. And there is the issue of Liam needing Mom's car, but maybe if we're working different schedules it wouldn't be a problem. Rafferty's is a nighttime thing.

"Lucy!" Hank screams my name from the upweller.

"I gotta get back. Thank you so much for doing this."

"No problem. It looks like Chloe has retrieved her treasure-hunt booty, so I'm going to take off, but I'll be in touch."

I turn sideways in my shell, and this time I high-five Chad. "Thanks, again!"

He smiles and waves before he leaves to catch up with his sister and Chloe, and I realize for the first time in weeks, I'm happy and excited to have a new plan. Usually, I never operate without one. Who knew good things could happen when you spill your shell to a stranger?

Chapter 19

"Horseshoe crabs breed under a full or new moon. It sounds romantic, but it's their ability to adapt that has kept these ten-legged creatures on this planet for more than three hundred million years. Love never got in the way of their survival."

From "What's Love Got to Do with It? The Dating and Mating Habits of North American Sea Life." A junior thesis by Lucy Giordano.

That night Mom and Dad insist we all sit down together for a pasta dinner. Thankfully, Dad did the heavy lifting with this meal. Mom can boil water and throw in spaghetti from a box, but Dad makes his marinara sauce from scratch, letting it simmer on the stove for hours with sausage and home-made meatballs.

"This is awesome, Dad," I say.

"Good job with the pasta, Mom," Liam says, not to be out-done. "I like it al dente."

Halfway through a rather silent meal, our family dinner turns into a family meeting. Dad tells us his plan for storing our per-sonal items when the renters move in. What we don't bring to

Gram's will get put in the attic or in our closets, which will be locked and off limits to the tenants.

"When does all this have to be done by?" Liam asks.

"They move in the first weekend in August, so I'd say the last weekend in July for the bulk of it. Whatever fits in your suitcases can wait until the last minute," Dad says.

"The thought of people sleeping in my bed gives me the heebie-jeebies," I say.

"For once, I'm with Lucy," Liam agrees.

"I'm buying mattress covers, and if it bothers you both so much, you're free to spend your summer job money on new mattresses," Mom says.

The internship Chad told me about is sounding costlier than I thought. It will cut into my Breakwater Burrito hours and cost me gas money, but like he said, it would be worth it for the chance to work with mammals next summer.

"That reminds me," I say. "I'm applying for an internship at the Marine Mammal Stranding Center."

"All the way down by Atlantic City?" Mom asks in a way that indicates she doesn't approve.

"Paid?" Dad asks.

I shake my head and he grimaces.

"How are you going to get there?" Liam asks. "You don't have a car."

"Neither do you," I fire back.

"I was planning on using Mom's car to get to work. You know that."

I suppose this is the point where the family meeting turns into the family argument.

"So? Andrew can drive you if I need the car. We can share it. Right, Mom?"

"If Lucy gets the job and you both get your licenses, we'll talk about it. There's nothing to discuss right now."

Oh, but Liam begs to differ. "You're amazing, Luce. You know that? You knew I needed that car for work, and now all of a sudden you're interested in driving sixty miles for an unpaid internship."

"Well, if I'd gotten the Sedge Island internship it wouldn't have mattered, but I didn't. Besides, this just came up today. I met a guy who interned there."

"Another guy? Two aren't enough?" Liam looks appalled. Like I've just announced I'm pregnant and may need a paternity test. Asshole. Saying crap like that to me in private is one thing, but in front of our parents? I stand up to leave.

"Shut your stupid mouth, Liam."

"Right, I'm the stupid one. You love that, don't you? At least I left prom with the person I went with."

"At least I left sober!"

"That's enough!" booms Dad.

"I'm going to my room," I say.

"Don't bother. I'm leaving," Liam says.

"Both of you are going to stay right here and clean these dishes," Mom says. "Your father and I are the ones who are leaving. This kitchen better be spotless when we get back from our walk."

"I'm disappointed in both of you," Dad says. "I'm starting to think neither of you will get to use the car this summer."

Liam shoots me a look that would turn Medusa to stone, but I don't care. My parents walk out the front door and I half expect him to bolt, but he helps me clear the dishes and wash the pots and pans. We stay out of each other's space while we work, neither wanting or daring to get close enough to breathe in the other's anger. I don't like the way the silence settles between us and wish we could finish the argument we started at dinner and move on. A couple of times I almost say something. But Liam finishes drying the pasta pot, throws the towel against the drying rack, and bolts out the back door. Watching him leave is something I'm getting used to.

Up in my room I survey the furniture and walls, making mental notes of what I'll need to pack away. Taped to my mirror are the photo-booth pics of me, Kiki, and Meghan, a few pictures of me and Liam surfing, and my favorite—one of me and Andrew. My sunrises and sunsets can stay up, but these are personal. I wonder if I'll be putting these back up when we return on Labor Day.

I'm about to open my laptop and check my email when my phone dings with an incoming text. At first I think it might be Connor. I haven't heard from him since Friday. I check the screen. Andrew. Saw you today. Dressed like a clam and surrounded by minions. I text back. Part of my plan to take over the world. Andrew texts back a smiley face. I wait for a few minutes to see if he has more to say. Maybe he's waiting for me? So I type. Taking oysters to Sedge next Sunday. Want to come? Andrew came with us last spring and was a big help.

Five minutes go by without an answer, and I second-guess my decision to put myself out there. Why did I bother? Because I miss our friendship, and I'm not sure how to get it back.

I'm stuck—stuck dealing with the consequences of two impulsive decisions involving Connor; stuck by myself when I should be with my friends; stuck wondering which guy I'm meant to be with. I think about Madame Ava's observation about the right boy at the wrong time. I just assumed she meant Connor, but the comment could have just as easily been about Andrew. You know what? I don't care. I'm tired of thinking about Andrew and Connor. I don't want to be stuck. I want to be the one doing the deciding.

I flip open my laptop and I'm thrilled to see that Chad has already been in touch. He sent me the name of the contact at the stranding center, along with a list of colleges around the country that offer marine biology majors. That was nice of him, but I'm planning on staying in New Jersey and getting my undergrad degree in biology. He also copied me on the email he sent to the center's contact person, explaining who I was and that I'd follow up.

I reply to Chad's email, thanking him profusely, then spend some time crafting the perfect response to the stranding center's director of interns. It's after eight on a Sunday, so it's not like I'd expect to hear back tonight. But at least my email will be waiting there on Monday morning. Maybe I'll check out the list of colleges Chad sent, just for the heck of it. But first, I need a snack.

I'm rummaging around in the kitchen pantry when I hear laughter coming from the yard. Andrew. I crack open the porthole-sized window at the rear of the pantry. It's up high and faces the yard, so I can hear without being seen.

"Hey, how much do I owe you for those tickets?" Andrew asks.

"Ask Kiki. She got them for me for my birthday," Liam replies.

"For Meghan and Mateo too," Kiki says. "She'll be home by then."

Liam and my friends are making birthday plans without me? Plans that require tickets? I guess I'll be asking Adela if I can work until close on my birthday. Dad's taking us for our driving test that morning. But stupidly, I was keeping the night free. My cheeks flush with embarrassment. *You're such an idiot, Luce.* Of course things won't be back to normal by then.

More laughing drifts in from outside, and for the next few minutes their words sound like distant mumbling, like they're moving away, until Andrew yells: "I'm taking off, man!" His voice comes through the side kitchen window by the Malloys' driveway.

No longer hungry, I abandon my snack search and sprint

back up the stairs to my room, where I grab my laptop and start researching the colleges on Chad's list. There're two in Florida, three in California, and one in North Carolina. Princeton is my dream school, but even if I can get in, I doubt we'll be able to afford it.

Rutgers has always felt like the best and obvious choice for me. I never wanted to be too far from home, but "home" isn't quite what it was last summer—and who knows what or where it will be a year from now. Maybe it's time to consider exploring out-of-state colleges where, from a distance, I'll hardly notice that everyone here has walked away.

Chapter 20

"After a complicated courtship, female sea horses 'impregnate' males by depositing eggs into their kangaroo-like pouches. Daddy sea horses then attach themselves to a plant or rock while their bellies expand and they await their brood's birth."

From "What's Love Got to Do with It? The Dating and Mating Habits of North American Sea Life." A junior thesis by Lucy Giordano.

I sleep only two hours that night but still manage to have a nightmare. In it, my brother and friends are all going someplace without me. They're dressed up, like they were for prom. I'm dressed like a clam but for some reason decide to follow them, even though it's impossible to be stealthy in my costume. They take a limo, and I drive myself in Mom's car, the whole time thinking, *How are my hands reaching the steering wheel?*

I tail the limo until it finally arrives at a church—a big cathedral with ornate arches and steep steps leading up to its carved wooden door. I wait for my friends to go inside, then follow. Climbing the steps is like walking up a down escalator, but eventually I get to the top. I walk through a first set of doors and plan to open the second set a crack to peek inside. But then blaring trumpet music starts and the doors fly open and I'm staring at a church full of people. Connor is at the top of the aisle, looking amazing in a tux. I think he's staring at me, and I'm totally embarrassed, but then I realize he's looking behind me so I turn around and see Bryn in a wedding gown.

I wake, my hair soaked with sweat and plastered to the side of my face, and can't fall back to sleep. By 5:00 a.m. I give up trying. I pull on jean shorts and a tee, grab a quilt from my closet, and walk to the beach. As I step through the dunes, I breathe deeply and fill my lungs with salty air. I'll miss its familiar scent when we return to Gram's. Summer isn't summer and breathing isn't breathing without it. *How will I survive at college without an ocean?* I wonder. Rutgers isn't on the coast, but some of the colleges on Chad's list are. Just not this coast.

The sky brightens as I watch members of the Sunrise Yoga Club set up their mats by the water's edge. A few people wrapped in blankets sit watching the horizon. Either they managed to evade the police and slept here all night, or they got up early like me and the yoga people. I walk north on the beach toward what used to be the pier and find a spot where I can be alone. The horizon is clear, which means it's going to be an awesome sunrise. I'm glad I brought my digital camera with me. It has telephoto and wide-angle lenses, and takes much better pics than my phone.

I stare at ocean, and let the rhythm and rumble of the waves consume me. I don't want to think about Connor not calling, Andrew not answering my text, or my friends and Liam leaving me out of birthday plans.

A tangerine speck peeks over the line where the water meets the sky and my heart jumps. I squish my toes in the sand and balance my camera on one knee to frame the shot. The orange speck rises skyward like a hot air balloon, and I begin clicking. Once the sun makes its appearance, it rises quicker than one might think. Experience has taught me to be ready and not turn away. The egg-yolk-colored sun, now a half-circle on the horizon, turns the sky yellow and paints a golden trail along the waves. Two seagulls dip in front of the giant orb as they fish for breakfast. *Click.* That's the keeper.

The last time I watched the sunrise, I was with Andrew and Izzy. It was January, not long after his family had moved back to Seaside after the storm, and the same day we became a couple. I'd spent the previous day at Andrew's house, and Izzy had begged me to stay over.

"You should," Andrew said. "We'll get up early and watch the sunrise over the ocean."

"Me too?" Izzy asked.

"If it's okay with your parents," I told her. "Bring your camera."

We had to sneak onto the beach the next morning. It was still closed and the overnight pedestrian curfew, meant to protect the town from looters, had not yet been lifted. Izzy had never watched the sunrise over the Atlantic, and she raised her hands and cheered at that first golden glimpse.

The air felt raw against my cheeks, but the ocean was calm, with gentle, rolling waves and hardly any whitecaps. It didn't look like winter. Andrew put his arm around my shoulder and said, "From here it all looks the same. Like nothing ever happened." Andrew always knew how to make everything all right. I rested my head on his shoulder, and Izzy snapped a picture of us from behind: our chiaroscuro silhouettes watching the dawn of a new day. Andrew made me a print—the one in my room waiting to be boxed up, maybe for good.

I wait until the sun climbs a bit higher in the sky before walking back toward the beach entrance where I slip my sandy feet into my blue flip-flops and head for home.

· • ● • ·

On Thursday afternoon I'm just finishing my shift at Breakwater Burrito when Chad walks in with Chloe, his sister, and the baby, only this time Chad's the one wearing the carrier. It's odd but endearing.

"I hope you don't serve clam tacos and oyster burritos," Chad jokes.

"No mollusks on the menu." I smile.

"How many jobs do you have anyway?"

"Just this one. The clam thing is only once a week."

Chad's sister extends her hand. "I'm Candace. Thanks for chasing down Chloe the other day."

Guess they're all about "C" names in their family, whereas we're partial to ones beginning with "L," I think as I shake her hand. "Lucy. I would have gotten to her sooner had it not been for the shell."

She pats the carrier with the tiny sleeping infant inside. "Tell me about it. Most days I feel like a kangaroo. My little bro is giving me a break today."

Hmm. I wonder if Liam would sport a baby carrier for me. Yeah, right. Not if it required speaking to me.

I take their orders, and as Chad pays he asks, "Heard anything from the stranding center?"

I better get my butt in gear and learn how to parallel park, or I'm going to be the one who's stranded, I think. "Not yet."

"Give it a week. If you haven't heard by then, I'll reach out to them for you."

"Thanks! I will."

Kiki arrives while I'm gathering my stuff in the back and getting ready to go. She opens her mouth like she's about to say something, but I don't have time for her right now. I want to talk to Chad before he leaves, and I'm not even close to being over her buying concert tickets for all our friends for Liam's birthday—for my birthday. It's like she just assumed we wouldn't be friends again.

I walk over to Chad's table. He and Candace look like they're done eating, but Chloe is taking her time with her chicken strips and chips. "Hey, I just wanted to let you know Reclam Our Waters is taking some oysters out to Sedge Island on Sunday if you're still around. You're welcome to join us. After the oysters are dropped, we're going to do some kayaking."

Chad looks like he's seriously considering it. "I've always wanted to go out there. Maybe I will."

"The boat launch is down about seven miles on the right. You can't miss it. We're leaving at nine in the morning."

I want to add that it's all in the name of science, not a date, but I'm pretty sure Chad knows my love life is a mess and he doesn't seem the type to creep on underage girls.

"Cool," Chad says. "Maybe I'll see you."

I sense Kiki watching me as I leave, but I don't care. From a distance, I'm sure Chad looks like one half of a young couple with kids, not some guy I'd be interested in. *Nothing to see here, Keeks, nothing to see.* I almost laugh to myself as the screen door bangs behind me.

Chapter 21

"When female harbor seals lack enough suitable places to raise their pups—pupping, it's called—they tend to all gather in one area. Unfortunately, tight quarters mean females get monopolized by large groups of males during mating season. Life for single seal ladies is definitely not like a Beyoncé song."

From "What's Love Got to Do with It? The Dating and Mating Habits of North American Sea Life." A junior thesis by Lucy Giordano.

Aside from the brief stint at Gram's, I have lived my entire life equidistant from the bay and the ocean. My moods depend on the tides. The ocean is my loud, my crazy, my scary, my thrill, sometimes all at once. But the bay? The bay is my calm, my quiet, my steady, and Sedge Island is the place where I get lost in the Zen of simple tasks—seining for silversides, hunting for starfish and horseshoe crabs, kayaking at sunset. It's the place where I go to hear my own thoughts. Not today.

Today my only thought is: *this will end badly*. Like, *Survivor* meets *Lord of the Flies* with a splash of the *Bachelorette* badly.

I'm sitting between scowling Andrew and silent Connor at the back of the pontoon boat, which is taking us to Sedge Island. All three of us are facing Chad, who chose to stand. Thank goodness there are some camp kids on board. They're a good distraction, chatting away with nervous excitement as they take in the bay's beauty and shoot video with their phones.

"How long is this boat ride anyway?" screams the kid next to Andrew.

The wind and motor make it hard to hear.

"Fifteen minutes!" I shout back.

Fifteen minutes that right now seem longer than the unedited version of *Titanic*. We're less than a mile offshore on a sparkling summer morning, but with the look of impending doom on our faces (Not Chad's—he seems amused.), you'd think we were lost in the North Atlantic.

"Who is that dude anyway?" Andrew asks me, nodding toward Chad.

"I told you when I introduced you. He's a marine conservation major at Rutgers. I was standing with him the day you blew by on your skateboard without saying 'hello.' Remember?"

"You were a giant clam. I remember."

"I didn't know you'd be here. You never replied to my text." I'm trying not to raise my voice, but it's hard to be heard over the engine.

"And I didn't realize you'd turned oyster restoration into *The Dating Game*."

I turn toward Connor and roll my eyes. He nods his chin

toward Andrew as if to say, "What's going on?" to which I mouth: "Tell ya later."

The boat docks and I wait for the kids to disembark first. They're with the Audubon Society camp and will be spending the entire week in the bunkhouse. Judging from their height, complexions, and overall awkwardness, I'd say they're about thirteen years old. I remember the July I became a teenager, how awkward and emotional I felt all the time. I wanted to go back to being twelve, to our safe and cozy elementary school and a time when summers seemed to last forever. Even now, there's something very appealing to me about never growing up. Though this island has magical qualities, it's not Neverland.

On the dock, Reclam Our Waters volunteers discuss taking two smaller boats out to the reef to offload the bushels of year-old oysters, but I decide to stay behind and manage the mess I've created. I should never have invited all three guys, but when Connor arrived late last night without Bryn, he texted to say he wanted to talk.

I was already in bed, and at the time, I didn't think Chad or Andrew would be showing up so I invited Connor to Sedge today. Last summer I promised to take him kayaking, and this seemed like the perfect opportunity. Poor Chad is caught in the middle of all my bad planning, so I introduce him to Hank, hoping he'll take Chad out on the oyster boat with him. I want Chad's day to be worthwhile.

"Chad's a marine conservation major at Rutgers and interested in what we're doing," I say. "Maybe he can tag along?"

"Sure," Hank says. "He looks strong. He can help us lift the oysters."

"I'd love to," Chad says.

"Don't worry. There'll still be plenty of time for kayaking. The reef isn't that far," I tell him.

His eyes pan from Andrew to Connor, who are both standing near the bunkhouse. Connor is wearing a plain white tee and cargo shorts. Andrew's in his usual gray plaid shorts, which accentuate his buttlessness, and a black Ramones T-shirt that I've never seen before. They look like yin and yang standing next to each other. They do not look like friends, and yet they've both become more than friends to me.

"Sure you don't need me to stay?" Chad asks. "I can go all big brother on those two if you need."

"You've already helped a lot. Sorry for the mix-up today."

He puts a hand on my shoulder. "Are you kidding? I wouldn't have missed this. Oysters really are an aphrodisiac. Who knew?"

I smile. "Thanks for understanding."

I step down from the dock unsure what to do first or who to do it with. There's no way the three of us are going kayaking together. As I join Connor and Andrew at a picnic table, I'm beginning to share Liam's view that life here is too constricting. More space would be nice right now.

I'm trying to think of something to say when a camp counselor walks up to Connor. "Can you help me get the kayaks off the rack and onto the beach while the kids are settling into the bunkhouse?"

"Whatever you need," Connor offers.

"Follow me," the counselor says.

"*Whatever you need*," mimics Andrew as soon as Connor is out of earshot. "Is that what he said on prom night when you took off with him?"

I scowl. I didn't think we were going to do this here and now, but if that's what Andrew wants, I'm sooo ready.

"Gee, I don't know, Andrew. Is that what Stacie said to you? Do you not remember why I wanted to leave?"

"Do you not remember me asking for one more night?"

I shake my head. "I'm not going to let you do that."

"Do what?"

"Turn it around on me. How was more time supposed to change things? You were the one with a girl in your lap. How do you think I felt when I saw you?"

"Well, I suppose you felt like leaving with another guy. Just tell me, is Liam right? Did you cheat on me?"

"God, Andrew. I didn't cheat on you. I would never cheat on you. Liam doesn't know what he's talking about. He's always hated Connor."

"Maybe he has good reason. Connor kissed his girlfriend."

"His *ex*-girlfriend, and when did you become so tight with Liam, Andrew? Huh?"

"Since he was the one who stayed at prom, Lucy. You bailed. On all of us."

"You bailed on me first! With Stacie. Are you going to deny that you have feelings for her?"

"I don't have to deny anything. You and me. We aren't together anymore, right?"

His words sting. "I knew you liked her. You've liked her for months."

Andrew lets out an exasperated groan. "Don't you get it? I've liked you my whole life. We get each other. Don't we owe it to each other to try again? I miss you."

Holy three-sixty, Batman. He's making me dizzy.

"Right. You miss me so much that you made plans to spend my birthday with Liam and our friends. I don't remember spending one birthday without you, Andrew. Not one. Is that how much you miss me?"

"How did you…"

"I heard you, Andrew. And Kiki too. In the yard the other night. That's what you wanted, right? For me to find out? To punish me? Maybe we both messed up on prom night, but I'm the one being blamed. You were the closest person in the world to me, closer than Liam even. I don't know what we owe each other, Andrew. But a phone call would have been nice. You haven't spoken to me in sixteen days. You passed right by me when I was standing in the middle of the street dressed like a clam. Who does that?"

"Luce, you're right—" Andrew reaches for my hands but I pull them away.

"Why don't you find the camp people and see if you can make yourself useful? I'm going to help Connor with the kayaks."

I stomp off and leave Andrew standing there. My grand speech and exit might have been more effective if I'd left the clam costume out of it. Maybe Andrew will take the next boat off the island. He can swim back for all I care. I walk around the bunkhouse to where Connor is lining up kayaks on the shore and begin taking paddles off the rack.

"Everything okay?" Connor asks.

I nod. My eyes are filled with tears. I'm afraid if I talk I'll start to cry. Thankfully the Audubon counselor, whose name I don't know, walks out of the bunkhouse with six kids in tow—four girls and two boys.

"You two mind helping me with a kayaking demo?" he asks. "Your pal Andrew over there agreed to help teach the other group to seine."

"Sure," I say. This wouldn't be the first time I've helped out with a camp group while on Sedge. It stinks that I won't be working here, but the letter said they had double the usual number of applicants and first preference went to those with college credits.

After a brief tutorial in how to hold the paddle (if it's upside down, you'll never go in a straight line) and turning (paddle on the left to turn left, on the right to turn right), the kids are ready to hit the water—and so are Connor and I.

I help pairs of kids wade into the water and get into their two-person open kayaks. "Remember!" the counselor yells from his one-man kayak a few yards out on the water. "If you stand in the kayak, you will fall and we will laugh. Do not stand in the kayak. Do not lean too far to one side either. Unless you want to go swimming."

Then he leads the pack of first-time kayakers away from the shore toward the water trails through the marsh. It's a bit like a corn maze, only you're on the water, in a boat, and surrounded by tall swamp grass and reeds instead of corn. Connor and I bring up the rear in our own kayak and I'm up front, so Connor will have to mirror my paddling.

"Do you want to talk about what happened with Andrew?" he asks after we've gotten a good rhythm going and the kids have all settled into a comfortable pattern in front of us.

I hesitate, wondering how much to share. "It's messed up. He started off telling me how he's still mad at me for leaving the junior prom with you and that I abandoned all my friends. Then two seconds later he's saying that he wants me back." My voice almost cracks.

"Back as a friend or more?" He sounds worried.

"I'm honestly not sure. More, I think."

"What do you want?"

"I don't know." I have to admit, there are more pros than cons to getting back together with Andrew.

"I know it's been hard on you. And I get why he's pissed, but what's the deal with your other friends?" Connor says.

"Keeks and Meghan said I ruined their night. And Liam…"

"Pfff. Liam. We know what that's about. He's never going to like me, is he?"

Maybe it's time I brought this up. "Hooking up with his ex-girlfriend didn't help."

"Natalie? It was one kiss."

I hold up one hand. "I don't want details."

"There are no details! Is that why Liam didn't tell you I called?"

"It was a factor."

He doesn't say anything after that for a while. The gentle splash as our paddles hit the water is the only sound. Maybe he's considering the downside to kissing every girl who crossed his path. Finally I say, "Let's not talk about Liam and Natalie. What's going on with you? When does your job start?"

"I start on Monday. I'll be framing a house in Ortley."

That's the town just north of the boardwalk, which was one of the hardest hit.

"I think that's awesome, Connor. Really. How cool is it that you know how to build houses? What about Bryn? What's she doing this summer?"

"Working at her mom's law firm."

"Is she coming down for the Fourth?"

"Don't know. If she is, she's not staying with me."

Do his parents not want her around? "What? Why?"

"We're done," he says.

I stop paddling for a second and turn as much as I can to look at Connor. "Done? Since when?"

"Since before we started. But officially since yesterday. Right before I left. I told her it would be best if she didn't come down for the Fourth. Told her it would be best if we didn't see each other at all anymore."

"And she was okay with that?"

"Honestly? She acted all pissed at first because I was the one who ended it, but by the end of the conversation, I could tell she was relieved. She's leaving for college soon. I don't think either of us thought it was going to last. We both knew we were kind of using one another to get over someone else."

"Who were you trying to get over?"

The bay makes soft lapping noises against the side of our orange kayak. A great white egret emerges from the tall grass and takes flight. My eyes follow him upward, toward the hazy summer sky.

"Luce. Did you think that day meant nothing to me?"

I don't want him to ask me that question. I want him to tell me that day meant everything. Because that's what it meant to me. *Everything*. But I can't bring myself to say that, not yet.

"Do you think we can get back there again?" he practically whispers.

I stop paddling. Dragonflies light on the brackish water, then take off into the grass. The kids giggle somewhere off to my right, making me long for the days when I could be silly. I swivel in my seat and reach for him, and he takes my hand. We stay that way for a while, letting the current carry us.

Chapter 22

"For male Eastern box turtles, the decision to mate cannot be taken lightly. Once copulation begins, the turtles can stay coupled for up to three hours.

Afterward, males sometimes fall on their backs and die of starvation if they can't right themselves. What a way to go."

From "What's Love Got to Do with It? The Dating and Mating Habits of North American Sea Life." A junior thesis by Lucy Giordano.

Chad and I spend Monday morning surfing. I felt bad about dragging him into my island adventure yesterday and told him to meet me at the Second Avenue beach if he was around. Connor left before dawn for his *Restore the Shore* work, and Andrew was back to not speaking to me so I knew there'd be no chance of drama.

"So, do you have big plans for the Fourth?" I ask him while we're toweling off.

We usually go to the Clarks', but this year I don't think I'm welcome. Plus, Mom wants us to be together since Liam's going out the next night on our birthday.

"That depends on whether or not you consider proposing to your girlfriend big plans."

His words give me chills. "Holy crap, that's huge! I didn't know you had a girlfriend."

"Six years. We've been together since we were fifteen. My sister helped me pick out the ring."

"Wow," I say. "I mean...wow." I'm simultaneously happy and terrified for Chad. Marriage is huge, and it sounds nice, but it's never been a goal for me. Straight As, internships, college, a career... What would it take for marriage to make that list? "Are you sure?"

"I know, right? It's crazy. I think we're kind of young, but I don't care. I can't imagine my life without her."

I like Chad's answer. People should get married only if they're lucky enough to find a person they can't live without. "So how'd you two meet?"

He laughs. "We met in pre-K," he says. "Elise let me borrow her scissors on the first day of school."

"Sounds like me and Andrew."

"The skateboarder?"

"Yeah. We've been friends since preschool too. Then we were more, and now...it's complicated. Did you always like Elise?"

"Well yeah, but not that way. Not until our sophomore year in high school. Then 'like' turned into 'like like,' then love."

"But how did you know you were *in* love? Friends can love each other."

"I just knew. Like knowing a wave is perfect before it's fully formed. You feel it on some other level. You just know."

I nod, remembering times I've felt that way and knowing it wasn't because of Andrew.

"How about you?" he asks. "Which boy from the island is going to get the rose?"

I laugh. "Neither. I think I'm better off alone."

"Oh come on. At the ripe old age of… How old are you again?"

"I'll be seventeen on Friday."

"At the ripe old age of 'seventeen on Friday' you've decided to become a curmudgeonly spinster?"

I kick some sand at his feet. "Hey, that's offensive! I'm not a spinster. I just don't want a boyfriend right now. Clams, work, and waves. I'm good."

I grab my bag and board and get ready to leave. Chad does the same.

"Sounds like you've got a plan."

"I do. And it doesn't include Connor or Andrew." I start walking toward the top of the beach, but Chad doesn't move. When I turn around, I can tell he's not finished talking about this.

"Let me ask you something: do you love to surf?"

I point to my board and raise my eyebrows.

"Okay, no need for facial sarcasm. Were you always this good at it?"

"Of course not. When I started I could barely stand up on my board."

"Did you fall a lot?"

"Yes."

"Get hurt?"

"All the time."

I start walking again, and Chad falls into step beside me.

"Did it make you afraid to get back out there?"

"Sometimes, but I had to get over it. Fear and surfing don't mix."

"So you didn't quit?"

I know where Chad is going with this. "No, I didn't quit."

"Of course you didn't because it's better to be out there getting our asses kicked than standing around watching."

"I think I read that in a fortune cookie once." Chad gives me a friendly shove and we both start laughing.

My phone rings as we're leaving the beach. It's a number I don't recognize but I pick it up anyway. I lay my board down so I can talk.

"Hello? This is she. Really?... Yes, of course I'm still interested and available... Uh-huh...uh-huh...sounds great. A week from today? Absolutely. I'll be there. Thank you. Thank you so much!"

Chad waits patiently until I'm off the phone. "I got the internship at the stranding center!" I shriek after I disconnect. Without thinking, I give him a hug. "I owe you."

"You don't owe me a thing. You're perfect for it."

"I start a week from today." My smile fades when the reality hits me.

"Is that a problem?"

"It won't be if I get my license on Friday. I haven't been behind the wheel in forever, and I have no idea how to parallel park."

"Take your board home. You're coming with me."

"What, where?"

"You're going to learn how to parallel park."

Ten minutes later, Chad pulls up in front of my house in an SUV with his board on top. He gets out of the driver's seat and walks around the car. "You drive."

I get in, adjust the mirrors, and click my seat belt. "Are you sure you want to risk this?"

"It'll be good practice for when I'm a dad."

"Don't tell me you're already thinking about kids!"

"Not until I'm, like, thirty. But yeah, someday. It's the next logical step."

"That implies that asking someone to marry you is also a logical step," I say.

Chad considers this. "You're right. Neither step is logical. But love is an inexact science. Or maybe it isn't a science at all."

Chad's right. Love isn't science at all. I know it's not biology. I thought maybe it was chemistry. It's not even gravity. But what is it then? Fifteen minutes into my lesson, I'm convinced love and parallel parking have a lot in common. There are tense moments and blind spots, and times when I can't see the curb at all. But then some mysterious force guides me and I find I'm right where I was meant to be.

"Woo-hoo, you nailed it," Chad yells when I get it right after only three attempts.

I put the car in park and look around. A perfect fit and yet I don't know how I got here or whether or not I can do it again.

I give Chad another hug when he drops me off at my house. Turns out, my day with him was one of the best I've had all summer. He's smart, easy to talk to, and a patient teacher.

"Good luck on Thursday. I want to hear how you ask Elise and what she says," I say.

"You got it. Good luck with your driver's test and the job. You're going to be great, Lucy. I know it."

He gets into his car and rolls down the window. "I don't really think you're a curmudgeonly spinster."

"That's nice of you to say. I still think you're a total science nerd."

Chad smiles. "I'll take that as a compliment." He's so familiar for someone I just met. Like the twin I should have had.

"It is."

"Remember. Whatever you're afraid of? Get over it. Love and fear don't mix."

And just like that, he drives away. Who knows when and if I'll see Chad again? I love that it doesn't matter. He and I hung out all day and it didn't have to mean anything. Girls inject so much emotion into everything. Chad made me miss having a guy for a best friend, and I realize now that Andrew and I should never have been more. It's not like I expected to be everything to Andrew for forever, but it would have been nice to have had his full attention for one lousy five-hour prom. Obviously I wasn't enough for Andrew, and maybe—probably—he wasn't enough for me.

I'm not sure what's next for me and Andrew and my friends. So many things got torn apart by the storm. Some got put back together the right way, some the wrong, others not at all.

Come September, where will I fit in? Thanks to Chad, I know now that I'm stronger than I thought. I'll get through it. Adapt or die. That *is* science and one of the first lessons I learned in biology. And it's so true. Ask any horseshoe crab. They've only been around for three hundred million years.

Chapter 23

"Size matters. Especially to male northern right whales who have the largest testes on the planet. When your family jewels weigh a ton, literally, one would think the bragging rights would be enough to win the unwavering devotion of a special lady. But the northern right whales' mating system is based on 'sperm competition,' and females copulate with multiple partners either in succession or at the same time."

From "What's Love Got to Do with It? The Dating and Mating Habits of North American Sea Life." A junior thesis by Lucy Giordano.

I haven't seen Connor since Monday when he started his job, but I hear him. His footsteps and truck, that is. He leaves super early and comes home late. I wonder if he's angry about our day on Sedge Island. He wanted more from me, I think. But I'm not ready. Not yet. He and Bryn are over, but I'm not over the intimacy they shared.

If I choose him over Liam and my friends, he'd become my world. I don't know if either of us is ready for that. It was a lonely two weeks after the prom when he went home and I had no one to talk to. What happens when summer ends? He'll have his life to go back to and I'll have my clams.

I finally run into Connor at the end of our block on the morning of the Fourth of July. He's on his way to the beach, and I'm on my way to work.

"Clams or tacos?" he jokes.

"Some of both."

"Do you ever slow down?"

"Not so much," I say. "I'm like a shark."

"Only much smarter."

It's crazy the way our conversations swing from serious to stupid small talk. "How's the house coming along?" I ask. Today it's stupid small talk.

"It's all framed. Tomorrow we start another one."

Tomorrow. That's right. My driver's test. My birthday. My friends and brother celebrating without me.

"How about you?" he asks. "How's work going? Any luck finding another internship?"

"That's right, you don't know. It happened so fast. I was going to mention it that day on Sedge but then… Anyway, I got an internship at the Marine Mammal Stranding Center. It's south of here. By Atlantic City?"

"Nice! I know how much you want to work with mammals."

"Chad hooked me up. He interned there himself."

"How is Chad?"

The way he asks makes me think he might be jealous. "Chad's getting married. He's proposing today."

His face brightens. "Good for Chad. I wish him the best."

"Me too." I glance at my phone. "Uh-oh, I've gotta run."

"Later?"

I move closer to him, then slip my arms around his neck and give him a hug. Connor seems surprised at first and tenses up, but then he relaxes, presses his body against mine, and hugs me back. I kiss him on the cheek and then we separate.

"Later," I say. "Definitely."

After a long afternoon at work—you know your food is good when you can lure people away from their Fourth of July barbecues—I walk in the back door to find Gram, Mom, and Dad gathered around the kitchen table. Liam is on his way out.

"Enjoy your cake," he says to me. "I've got plans. No one bothered to ask me if tonight was good for me."

Here we go. The fireworks *before* the fireworks.

"Mom planned this tonight because you won't be around tomorrow. Remember? You're going out with *my* friends."

"Wait just a second," Mom says. "I thought Lucy was going too."

"Hear that, Liam? Mom thought I was going too. Why aren't I again?"

"I don't have time for this. I'm going to Andrew's barbecue and then he's giving me a ride to work."

I like the way he managed to remind me I wasn't invited to the Clarks' this year.

"Liam, don't you talk to your mother that way," Dad booms.

"I was talking to Lucy, not Mom," Liam says, and then he walks out the front door and slams it behind him.

It's nice to see him slam a different door for a change, but I'm not going to lie, it hurts. How could it not? My brother hates me. I stand there, fists balled up, looking at the closed door.

"Why don't you sit down, sweetheart?" says Gram. "Have some cake."

Cake? I can barely swallow the knot in my throat, but I'm not going to take it out on my gram and parents like Liam did. "Sure, Gram. Just give me a few minutes. I'm going to change."

I'm in my room when I hear a light tap on the door. "Luce? Can I come in?"

Mom.

I wipe my eyes. I don't want her to see that I've been crying, not that it matters. I know she knows. That's why she came to check on me. Plus, it only takes one look in my mirror to confirm that my eyes are swollen and my skin is blotchy. I'm not a pretty crier.

"Come in," I call.

Mom opens the door slowly and quietly, as if I might have fallen asleep in the past three seconds, and peeks into my room. "Are you okay?"

"I'll be fine, Mom. Just give me another minute and I'll be down for cake. I don't want to disappoint Gram."

"It's okay, hon. Dad drove her home."

Gram hates to drive in the dark. She claims she has night blindness, but I think she's just nervous.

"I'm sorry. I didn't mean for Gram to leave."

"I think we have your brother to thank for that."

"He hates me." The words make my chest hurt.

"Lucy, don't say that. Liam loves you. He's just angry, which as we all know, isn't too unusual for Liam. Is this about prom night? Because he needs to get over it. That's between you and Andrew."

"It has more to do with who drove me home."

"Connor?"

I nod. "Liam hates him."

"Possibly," Mom says. "But I have a feeling he may have to get over that too."

I raise my eyebrows at Mom.

"Don't look so surprised," Mom says. "I'm a teacher, a lifeguard, and a mother of twins. I've been observing teen behavior longer than you've been on this planet."

"Liam has it in his head that I cheated on Andrew with Connor. And I swear—"

Mom holds up her hand. "I know you would never do anything like that. I'm afraid your brother is more like me—more guarded when it comes to outsiders."

Especially ones who hook up with your ex-girlfriend, I think.

"Mom, the Malloys aren't exactly outsiders. They've owned the house next door for a long as I can remember."

Mom sighs. "I know. But when I was growing up here, the people who owned that house rented it out for the entire summer. I had a habit of getting too attached to any kid who stayed next door. I wanted to make everyone my best friend, and when they left, I was always crushed. We'd exchange addresses and promise to write. I always did.

"Sometimes I'd get a letter back and sometimes I wouldn't. Every September I got depressed and my parents worried. Eventually they enrolled me in a junior lifeguard camp with other local kids and made sure I steered clear of the part-timers next door. Once my guard went up, I'm afraid it never came down."

"Except for Dad."

"True. Your father was different. He loved it here as much as I did. I had the feeling he wasn't going anywhere."

"I don't want to leave in August."

Mom puts a hand on my knee. "It's going to be hard, hon. But worth it if we're able to stay in the long run."

"Can I ask you something, Mom?"

"Of course. Anything."

"Do you remember who stood up on their surfboard first? Me or Liam?"

She's not surprised by the randomness of my question, nor does she have to think about it. "You. Why?"

"I always thought it was Liam. When we were little, it felt like he beat me at everything."

"I think that's because he tried to beat you at everything and you always let him."

I scrunch my face. Did I? I can't remember. "Really? Why would I do that?"

"Because you knew he needed to."

"I don't get it."

"Lucy, let me tell you something. You can be whatever you put your mind to. Your father and I never worried about what you could accomplish. Your brother, on the other hand, has always needed hand-holding and a cheering section for everything from potty training to trigonometry. I know it may seem like he gets extra attention from me, but that's only because he needs it. I teach the same way. I tend to focus on the kids who can't do a single sit-up, not the natural athletes."

I sigh and let my shoulders slump. "But even the natural athletes need to be told that they're doing a good job. That you value what they can do—what they can accomplish."

"You're right, honey." She sits on the bed, puts her arm around my shoulder, and draws me close. "I'm very proud of you. So is your father. We don't worry about you making the right decisions in life. We trust you."

Mom kisses my cheek then stands up. "How about we go downstairs and get some cake?"

"Sounds perfect. Just let me change out of my shirt. It smells like onions."

"Meet you downstairs. I'll cut two pieces for us."

"Okay."

She walks out the door then turns back. "One of the things I admire most about you, honey, is that you're as responsible as you are fearless. It's a rare combination."

And then the door clicks shut behind her.

Chapter 24

"When swans find their life partner, they engage in a tender courting ritual during which their wings quiver, their beaks touch, and sometimes their necks form a perfect heart."

From "What's Love Got to Do with It? The Dating and Mating Habits of North American Sea Life." A junior thesis by Lucy Giordano.

I wait until the town's fireworks display is over, then slip out the back door carrying my trusty quilt and one of Mom's hand-me-down lifeguard hoodies in a drawstring bag. As I walk down the boardwalk, the house comes into view one floor at a time, starting with the widow's walk, the balcony off the master bedroom, the wrap-around porch. I stop at a bench directly across from it. In the warm night, the air is heavy against my skin. Unlike the last time I saw this place.

The wind was crazy that day, lifting my hair and whipping it into my eyes as I walked toward the wrought-iron spiral staircase leading to the widow's walk. I remember that I placed my hand on the railing and hesitated for a moment before I took the first step. Connor followed close behind. His proximity made my knees shaky, but then I began the climb and never looked back.

Halfway up, I lost my footing, gasped, and stumbled backward, but Connor caught me just in time. My breath rushed to keep pace with my heart at the warmth and weight of his hands against my bare skin where my shirt had pulled away from my jeans. He steadied me as I climbed, and I knew his not letting go was about more than my safety. My cheeks were on fire when I reached the top.

Connor's hands fell away as I stepped onto the widow's walk. He stood by the staircase, and I moved to the center and spun around, giving the color in my face time to fade as I pretended to be absorbed with the view from all sides. The ride piers and water slides to the north, Island Beach State Park and the traffic circle to the south. The dense foreboding clouds blanketing the sky and making everything seem so heavy. I could feel Connor's eyes on me as I swept my hair to the side and tried to hold it in place. The unrelenting wind made it feel like we were on a ship, surrounded by angry water and headed for big trouble.

The bay was choppy, tossing around the few remaining boats still anchored near the shore. Toward the east, the ocean raged. I leaned against the railing and fixed my gaze toward the horizon. Eight- to ten-foot waves rushed the shore, pounding the surf in rapid succession and creating row after row of foamy whitecaps that matched the color of the thick, ominous clouds. The brightness made me squint, but I was still too afraid to look back at Connor. Afraid he'd see what being so close to him was doing to me.

"This is crazy," I yelled. "The storm's not even here yet."

"Crazy? I was thinking beautiful." Though there was plenty of room along the rail beside me, he moved to stand right behind me, so close I could feel the heat from his body.

"Beautiful and scary, you mean." I didn't think he'd heard me. The wind and ocean were louder than a jet engine. And yet when his fingertips laced with mine, the only thing I could hear was my own heart beating double time in my ears. *Chu-chu, chu-chu, chu-chu.* I angled my head to the side and raised my voice. "This is only low tide… The storm's going to make land-fall at high tide. During a full moon. People say it could mean a major storm surge. What do you think is going to happen?"

Connor closed the remaining space between us and bent his head toward my ear. "I know exactly what's going to happen."

The warmth of his breath sent chills down my neck and across my body. Every nerve ending pulsed. I turned to face him then. No boy had ever looked at me the way he did when he smoothed my hair away from my face, letting his fingertips linger as he traced my cheeks, my jawline, my neck. When he brushed my lower lip with his thumb, my lips involuntarily parted and I forgot to breathe.

I had to swallow hard before I could speak. "You know, wid-ow's walks became popular in North American coastal towns during the eighteen hundreds," I blurted out. "Wives of mari-ners would come up to these rooftop walks to watch and wait for their husbands to return from the sea. Although some say that's just a myth and these walks are merely a design element."

Connor raised his eyebrows and pretended to listen, but I could tell he hadn't heard a word I said. He was staring at my lips. "Is that so, Lucy Goosey?" Connor gave me a half smile as his eyes locked with mine and he ran a hand down my spine. As his fingers slid up under my shirt, touching the small of my back and pressing me against him, everything I'd ever felt for him came rushing to the surface. My legs trembled and I thought they might give out. All I could think was: *Is this swooning? This must be swooning.* I wrapped my arms around his neck to steady myself even though inside, I'd already fallen.

We stood there, each waiting to see where the moment would take us. I wanted to see him, to read him like he did me. The forceful wind pressed our clothes tight against our bodies, accentuating Connor's well-defined angles. I ran my hands down his torso, felt his muscles contract when I reached his waistband, then let my fingers move upward along his bare abs and chest before reaching around his sides and running my hands along his back.

Ah, that back. How many times had I stared at the broad, perfect shoulders that sloped into his muscular arms? I loved the color of his tanned skin. Connor pulled me close and rested his chin against the top of my head. Finally he spoke. "I've never known a girl like you before, Luce."

"Is that a good thing or a bad thing?"

He didn't answer. Instead, he lifted my chin and kissed me once, lightly, on the lips. "What do you think?"

It's like the kiss and Connor had asked the same question.

What did I think? I thought maybe he didn't know he had his arms around Lucy Giordano, the girl next door whose social skills were more suited to sand crabs and clams than boys. But Connor looked at me as if he knew exactly who I was, and he didn't wait for an answer. He bit his bottom lip, then kissed me again, deeper and longer.

I wrapped my arms around his waist as he cradled the back of my head, wrapping his fingers in my hair and holding on to me like he never wanted to let go. His kisses were soft, playful, sexy…making me half lose my mind and totally forget we were standing on a rooftop perch, fifty feet above Ocean Avenue with the storm of the century barreling toward us.

Connor Malloy was kissing me. I was kissing Connor Malloy. That's all that mattered. Everything else faded away— the metal hook clanging against the flagpole, the seagull's warning call, the morning church bells on Central Avenue. Connor tasted like sweetness and salt, as familiar to me as the ocean air. I couldn't believe he and I were together. After years of existing side by side, our orbits only intersecting occasionally, we'd finally collided. I wanted to stay wrapped in Connor Malloy forever.

The more we kissed, the more I feared the depth of my desire. *Could Connor sense how much I wanted this? How much I wanted him?* Finally, we pulled apart.

"I should probably get home," I said, even though leaving him made my chest ache.

He kissed me once more on the lips. "Mmm. I should probably lock up."

Still, neither of us made a move. I couldn't. Suddenly, I wasn't afraid of being needy or desperate. I didn't care about being late or being evacuated from my home. The thing I feared most was leaving Connor and having what we had just shared get washed away like it never happened.

I took his hand and walked toward the spiral staircase. "Come."

We wound our way down to the bedroom art studio. I stood behind him and kissed his neck as he locked the door, then we walked hand in hand to the main staircase. We got to the top and Connor paused, but I continued down the long, carpeted hallway toward the front of the house. When I turned, Connor stood dumbfounded where I'd left him. "Luce?" That was all he said.

"I think I'd like to see the view from the master bedroom now."

I waited at the doorway, holding my breath. When I felt his hands on my shoulders, his body close to mine, my grip tightened around the doorknob and I hesitated. Then Connor placed his lips against the back of my head and whispered: "Being here with you…it's like it was supposed to happen." I smiled but I didn't turn around. "It was," I said. Then I opened the door and we both walked inside.

Chapter 25

"Red-tailed hawks are monogamous, territorial birds that may mate for life. During breeding season, the pair performs a graceful air dance during which they link talons and spiral toward earth."

From "What's Love Got to Do with It? The Dating and Mating Habits of North American Sea Life." A junior thesis by Lucy Giordano.

I don't bother to text. I just call.

"Hey." Connor sounds drowsy. It gives me shivers. I could listen to sleepy, sexy Connor talk all night.

"Can you meet me at the beach?"

"When?"

"Now."

"I'll be right there."

By the time I arrive at the Second Avenue beach, Connor's waiting for me. He's sitting atop the badge checker's booth. Reclining, actually. He jumps off when he sees me and says, "Just posing for the camera."

"What camera?" I'm confused.

"You mean I know something about this place that you

don't?" He points up toward the light. "The beach cam. It's on Seaside's website," he says. "I figure it's up there someplace. I play it a lot. I like to study to the sound of the ocean."

"I had no idea it was there."

"Why would you? You can see the ocean from your bedroom window. I need my fix in the off-season."

"The ocean's not the best thing I've ever seen from my bedroom window."

Connor smiles and continues talking. "The ocean's not the best thing I've seen on the webcam."

"Huh?" I'm not sure where he's going with this.

"Last September, we had a few eighty-degree days and I remember thinking how badly I wanted to be here. So I turned on the webcam. I'd been watching for a few minutes when you walked right into the frame. You were standing right about here." Connor moves a step closer to the path leading down to the beach. "You turned your head up toward the camera and smiled, and I swear it felt like you looked right at me."

"Did it freak you out?" It's kind of freaking me out, although I don't know why. It's not like Connor installed the webcam to spy on me.

"Freak me out?" Connor laughs. "It made me want to tune in every day."

I bump his shoulder and smile. "FaceTime might have been more efficient."

"Nah. Too predictable. Seeing you on the cam that day was serendipity… It was like—"

I'm about to finish his sentence for him when a group of girls our age approaches. As we step aside to let them down the path to the beach, one of them says, "Connor?"

The words "It was supposed to happen" get lodged in my throat.

He squints at the gaggle of girls, like he's unsure where the voice came from. A petite brunette with facial piercings waves and smiles. "I thought that was you," she says.

"It's me, uh…"

Her smile fades. "Heather."

"Right, Heather. Well, uh, enjoy the beach."

"Yeah. You too." Heather does not sound happy. I can relate.

I watch where the girls go before I stomp down the path after them and head in the opposite direction. The fireworks are over, but I can hear the whistle and bang of firecrackers being set off further down the beach. Connor doesn't follow right away. He catches up to me as I'm spreading my quilt by the water's edge.

"Hey," he says. "Let me help you with that."

He bends down to grab a corner and straightens his side of the quilt. I can't look at him.

He walks over and takes my hands in his and tries to get me to make eye contact. "Please don't be mad at me. She just said 'hi.'"

Is this how it's always going to be? She just said "hi." It was just a kiss. She just followed me home. With girls and Connor, it's always "just" something it seems.

"I'm not mad at you. I'm mad at myself."

"For what?"

"For thinking we could work."

Connor moves his hands to my shoulders and touches his forehead to mine. "Luce, we can work."

"I'm not sure I can get past…your past."

"Everybody has a past, Luce. Look at you and Andrew. You two have shared something that you and I can never have."

"Friendship is different, Connor. That day at the house? You were—" I break off and take a deep breath, unsure how to go on. My heart beats fast against my ribs, like it wants out. "My history? It began with you." I have to turn away.

"Luce? Look at me." Connor lays a finger under my chin and turns my face toward him. His eyes penetrate mine, turn me inside out, and expose all the parts no one else sees. It scares and excites me and it only ever happens around him.

"First of all, *my* history? I'm not sure what you're thinking, but it isn't all that. Trust me. Who cares if some girl whose name I can't remember says 'hi'? None of that matters. It hasn't mattered since that day. I knew from the second I kissed you what I was starting. It doesn't matter if you weren't my first. I want you to be my last, Luce."

What do you say when the boy who has occupied your thoughts for the past year says exactly the right thing? Nothing. You kiss him. Softly at first, with my eyes wide open. Then with more urgency. I lay my hand on the back of Connor's neck and stroke his hair with my fingertips. His hands slide to my hips. We're pressed together and I can feel the rapid rise and fall of his chest, moving in time with my racing heart. Connor's lips travel from my mouth down my neck to my collarbone.

I take his hands and lead him toward the blanket, where he lies down and pulls me toward him. I kiss him again, brushing my lips along his jawline and neck. My hand travels across his chest, down his side, under his shirt… *This is what I wanted. This is why I called him tonight.* I want so badly to pick up where we left off last fall…and then I stop. I sit up straight on the blanket beside him. *This can't happen.* I want no mistakes this time. Big, small, or otherwise.

"Luce?" Connor puts a hand on my back. When I don't answer, he sits up too. "What's wrong?"

"I just don't want this part to end."

"What part?"

"The part where all we do is kiss. And go on dates. And talk on the phone every day. We haven't had this part yet."

He nods like he's still recovering from my one-eighty turn, then puts his arm around me and holds me tight. "You're right. This part doesn't have to end. It won't." He kisses my forehead, and I'm about to thank him for understanding when the alarm on his phone goes off and I jump. *Holy crap!* It sounds like an air-raid siren.

"Got someplace to be?" I ask.

Connor reaches for the pocket of his shorts and turns off the alarm.

"Yep. Right here. At midnight. Happy birthday, Lucy."

Tears prick my eyes. "You remembered."

"How could I not? I've been around for at least ten of them."

There's a small wrapped package in his hand. Connor hands it to me.

"What's this?" I ask.

"A puppy."

"Ha-ha," I say, but inside I'm a ball of goo.

"Just open it."

I do. It's a pearl necklace—not the grandma-ish kind or the ones brides wear. A single pearl wrapped in a knot pendant dangles from a black rope cord. I don't know what to say.

"I know oysters make pearls, not clams. But I thought a pearl would make a nicer necklace than a clam—"

I cut off his words with a kiss and feel the tension go out of his body.

He pulls back and smiles. "So you like it?"

"Like it? Did you ever see something and know instantly it was meant for you?"

Connor doesn't answer at first. Instead he wraps his arms around me and I collapse against his chest. He kisses me on the cheek and whispers in my ear, "Yes."

Chapter 26

"Manatees do not mate for life. During mating season the female (cow) may be followed by up to a dozen males (bulls) to form a mating herd, which facilitates indiscriminate copulation."

From "What's Love Got to Do with It? The Dating and Mating Habits of North American Sea Life." A junior thesis by Lucy Giordano.

I sleep through my alarm on my birthday and have to rush like a crazy person to get ready for my road test. Downstairs I find my brother already dressed and drinking coffee in the kitchen. It's like I've stepped into an alternate universe. "You missed Mom. She said we'll do presents later."

"Where's Dad?"

"In the car, waiting."

"All righty then." I touch my hair absently as we walk out the back door. I hope I have time to fix it before they take my picture. *If* they take my picture. My license means so much more now that I really need it.

At the Division of Motor Vehicles, Liam insists on taking the road test first. Actually, they should call it a parking-lot test because the test instructors don't really take you on the road. Instead, they ride shotgun with you as you drive around a small course with stop signs, yield signs, and orange cones for parking.

Dad and I sit in the DMV's uncomfortable plastic chairs and watch CNN on the flat screen while we wait for Liam. I'm more nervous than I thought. My internship depends on my being able to drive myself there, and getting access to the car depends on my strained relationship with Liam.

"I hope for all of our sakes he passes," I say.

"You read my mind."

I'm wearing a black tank top and jean shorts. I remembered mascara but forgot lip gloss. I'm going to be carrying this license for the next four years. I should have tried a tad harder. I take a ponytail holder out of my purse and run my fingers through my hair. Then I reach into my pocket, pull out the necklace Connor gave me, and slip it around my neck. I'm just closing the clasp when Liam returns. *Shit.* I see the look on his face and my heart sinks. Dad winces and shakes his head. It's going to be a long car ride home.

"You're up next," Dad says.

I breeze through most of the course, but my chest tightens when it's time to parallel park. I pull up next to the cones and take a deep breath. Last night's conversation with Mom echoes in my head. *You always let him win.* I could mess up my parallel parking, but what good would that do? Liam'll feel better for a day, but I'll lose my internship. How's that fair? Andrew already drives him to work. I put the car in reverse, give it a little gas, and maneuver between the cones on the first try.

"Well?" asks Dad as I walk in the front door of the DMV.

I hold up the slip from my test instructor.

"Of course," says Liam. "There's no such thing as a test Lucy can't pass."

"Liam," Dad says.

"Congrats, Luce." Liam looks deflated. He puts his hand on my shoulder, then walks outside. He's not going to make me feel guilty, not this time.

"Remain expressionless." That's what the guy who's about to take my picture tells me. *How do I remain expressionless?* I wonder when the flash goes off, causing me to look confused rather than devoid of emotion. Even the guy behind the counter thinks so. "Let's take one more." The retake isn't much better. What happened to my chin? My face looks shapeless, like a manatee.

The ride home is unbearably quiet. Liam got in the backseat and slammed the door, and I knew better than to ask Dad if I could drive.

"You'll take the test again in a week," Dad says. "That's not a long time to wait."

Liam doesn't say anything.

"We'll practice this weekend if you want."

More silence from the backseat.

My stomach clenches. I know I didn't have anything to do with Liam failing his road test, so why can I feel him blaming me?

"Why couldn't I have been an identical twin?" Liam says. "I could've borrowed Lucy's license and my friends could stop driving me around."

"So you're saying you wanted to be a girl?" Dad asks, trying to lighten the mood.

"No. I was thinking Lucy could have been a boy." He says it innocently enough, but I know it's a dig at my tomboy ways.

Liam could have been a girl. His mood swings give me vertigo, I want to snap, but I keep quiet and turn on the radio. It's a short drive, and I refuse to get sucked into a war of words with my brother.

At home, I text Mom our news. I don't want her blind-sided upon arriving home from work. Dad takes extra time making himself a sandwich to bring to work. I know he's afraid to leave us alone. So when Adela calls from Breakwater Burrito to see if I'd mind coming in—Keeks called in sick, which happens more often these days—my dad and I are both relieved.

"You don't mind working on your birthday?" Dad asks.

I shrug. "It's only eleven 'til five." It's not like I've got anything else going on. Connor's at work; Chad is back home and (hopefully) happily engaged; and my friends and brother—well…things there keep getting worse.

I arrive at Breakwater Burrito and Adela gives me a big hug. "Happy birthday, Lucia! So?"

I nod. Mac raises his hand for a high five. "Now you can drive to work, kiddo," he jokes.

"Yes, that three-block commute has been hell." I laugh.

My bosses' smiling faces, the sizzling onions, and the Beach Boys crooning about California girls make me forget the ride home from the DMV. The lunch rush has already begun. I jump on takeout register duty, and the next time I look at the clock, it's two and time for my break. Adela and Mac surprise me with cannoli cupcakes from the bakery, my favorite, and everyone sings "Happy Birthday."

My break is just about over when I get a text from Connor. Hey bday girl! Is it official? Can u drive tonight? I text back. Yes. :) Where are we going? He texts that it's a surprise. So is finding Andrew standing in the doorway.

I'm in the back by the kitchen, but I can see him panning the restaurant. My first instinct is to run, which is weird. In all the years I've known Andrew, I've never felt the urge to get away from him before. He's probably looking for Kiki. I'll bet he doesn't know she called in sick. But then he goes up to Jason, who's busing a table, and the next thing I know, Jason is pointing toward the kitchen, toward me.

Andrew walks over. "Hey, Luce. Happy birthday."

"Thanks," I say, and for some reason, I find myself blinking back tears. If only the sugar high from the cannoli cupcake could have lasted a little longer.

"Can we talk?"

"My break's kind of over." But Adela hears me as she squeezes past with more napkins and straws.

"Go ahead, hon. Take a few extra minutes. It's your birthday."

I lead Andrew out the back door. We stand about three feet away from each other, like it's a standoff at the O.K. Corral.

"I got my license," I offer. Not that he cares, but it's something to say.

"I heard."

Right. He and Liam are best buds now.

"I brought you something." Andrew hands me a card.

"Thank you." I hold it in my hands, not sure I want to open it in front of him. What if he wrote something weird or sad in there? I don't want to cry in front of him. Not anymore.

"Aren't you going to open it?"

"Should I?"

Andrew looks down at his feet and rolls a pebble under one sneaker. "There's a ticket in there. For tonight's all-ages show."

"Oh. Did Keeks cancel because she got sick?"

Andrew scrunches his eyebrows. "What? No. She's not really sick. She just wanted to hang out with Liam on his birthday. Your brother's really into her too. I didn't see that one coming, but I'm glad."

"Me too. I was afraid Keeks might get hurt. It took him a long time to get over Natalie."

"Some people are harder to let go of than others," he says quietly.

"Andrew—"

"So anyway, the ticket is from me. I'm sorry we left you out. I never should have let that happen."

I hand the card back to him. "I can't go, Andrew. Keeks and

I haven't had a civil conversation in weeks, and I've lost track of all the reasons Liam is pissed at me. No one wants me there."

"Screw them," he says. "Hang with me."

"What about Stacie?"

"What about her? She'll be there, but she has her own friends."

"Are you guys, you know, together?"

Andrew shrugs. "I'm not sure yet."

Part of me wants to go to the concert. To inch my way back to normal, at least where Andrew is concerned. But it sounds like Connor already made plans for us.

"Cool necklace," Andrew says.

My hand goes to my neck and I blush. I forgot I was wearing it. I nod.

"I was going to ask if it was a gift from your parents, but I can tell by the shade of pink you're turning, it's not."

I could lie, but what would be the point? Andrew already guessed. "Connor gave it to me." Andrew moves closer and looks into my eyes. "Keep the ticket. We'll be by to pick up Liam later. You too if you decide to go. 'Kay?"

"Okay." It makes me sad knowing I'm going to disappoint Andrew.

Andrew drops his arms and says: "I gotta go." And then before I can say anything more, he walks past the trash bins toward the street. "There're still tickets, you know. You can get them at the door. In case you want to bring someone else. Just sayin'." Then he gives me a quick two-fingered wave and walks away.

I open his card before going back inside. It has two little kids dressed in old-fashioned, too-big adult clothes. The little girl is wearing a floppy hat and white sunglasses, and the little boy sports a fedora askew on his mop of hair. He holds a yellow rose. I stare at the flower, the only splash of color in the black-and-white print. The inside of the card is blank except for Andrew's note. *Sorry that I screwed up at the prom. You were right about a lot of things. I don't know what we're meant to be, but I'm not letting go. Love, Andrew.*

My breath catches in my throat. I wipe my eyes with the back of my hand and go back inside. There I tuck the card in my bag, but Andrew's words stay with me for the rest of my shift.

Chapter 27

"Mating season for humpback whales is like a punk rock concert meets football. Long, involved songs are sung by the males to attract the ladies, and the fierce competition for females includes lunges, tail slashes, charges, and blocks."

From "What's Love Got to Do with It? The Dating and Mating Habits of North American Sea Life." A junior thesis by Lucy Giordano.

At home, I text Connor and tell him to call me after work. I totally respect him for volunteering all summer, especially since he gets paid to do the same kind of work for his father. My phone rings as I'm getting dressed.

"Ready for tonight?" he says when I pick up my phone.

"About that—"

I fill him in about the visit and ticket from Andrew. I leave out the card. That's between me and Andrew. "You should go, Luce," Connor says finally. "Make things right with your friends."

"I don't know. What if it's too weird?"

"Oh, it will be."

He's right. I try to picture hopping in the car with Liam and my friends, but I can't. "You're not helping."

"I'll go with you."

"It won't be weird for you?"

"We can handle weird together."

"Maybe we could just stop by…"

"Whatever you want is fine. Your birthday, your choice, Lucy Goosey."

It's the silliest nickname, but I love the way he says it and that he wants to be there for me when I face my friends. Maybe tonight will go better than I thought. It shouldn't matter, but having them accept that Connor and I are together would mean I could be the same person around them that I am with Connor. I could finally be me.

·•◉•·

The club is a few towns away from where we live and known for all-ages shows, featuring some pretty decent national acts. We had an all-ages club on the island, right on the beach, but the Atlantic Ocean plowed through it like a derailed freight train during Sandy and no one knows if it'll ever get rebuilt.

When Connor and I arrive, I'm nervous about what to expect. The bouncer stamps our hands after we give him our tickets. (The over-twenty-one crowd gets wristbands.) In general, I'm not very good at walking into dark, crowded rooms.

I've always relied on my point gals, Kiki and Meghan, but they were with Andrew when he picked up Liam, so I know they're already inside. Connor takes my hand and leads me through the crowd toward the bar.

The place isn't very big and I spot my friends immediately, pressed against the stage, where the first band is already playing. Andrew stands next to Meghan and Mateo, and all three of them are nodding their heads to the music. Liam and Kiki are off to the side. He stands behind her with his arms wrapped around her waist. My first reaction is "Ew." In theory, my brother and best girlfriend dating didn't seem like a bad idea. But now I realize I like it better without the visual.

I wasn't sure if I had the guts to come here up until the last minute. I left the house with Connor shortly after Mom and Dad presented Liam and me with gifts—gift cards, I should say. To the surf shop for both of us, the bookstore for me, and the music store for Liam. Before Liam went upstairs to get ready, he dropped the bombshell: "Andrew says I can stay with him in August."

"Oh?" Mom always says "oh" like a question when she's getting ready to shoot down an idea.

Liam played victim. "Since I don't have a license yet, it makes sense. Then you guys wouldn't have to worry about getting me to and from work."

"That's true," Mom says.

What? Was she actually caving?

"But isn't work closer to Gram's?" I couldn't help it. I had to chime in. "Anyway, we're not leaving yet. You'll have your license by then."

"I didn't hear me asking you, Lucy," Liam sniped. "You're just jealous because I'll be here and you'll be hanging with the over-fifty-five crowd at Leisure Village next month."

"I didn't hear us give you permission," Mom said.

"Your mother and I will discuss it," Dad said.

"Fine," Liam said before taking off for his room.

I can hear it in Dad's voice; they'll wind up letting him stay with Andrew. Who cares? It's probably best that we're apart for a while.

After Liam's grand pronouncement, I figured it was safe to tell my parents I was riding to the show with Connor. They exchanged a look, but thankfully didn't ask any questions before I retreated to my own bedroom. I didn't want to be downstairs when Andrew and my friends came to get Liam. I don't know if Andrew told my brother—or anyone else for that matter—that he invited me to the show, and I didn't want to be around when that tidbit was revealed.

But now here we all are. Together in one room for the first time since the junior prom.

I touch Connor's arm and nod toward my friends. "Wish me luck." I breathe deeply through my nose and am about to cross toward the stage when I see Stacie come up alongside Andrew. Mateo and Meghan see her and they each give her a kiss on the cheek, then Andrew puts a hand on Stacie's shoulder.

Have I been replaced? Not just as Andrew's girlfriend—I'd

already seen that one coming. But does my group of friends, my social safety net since preschool, now belong to Stacie? And my brother? Screw it. Even if it does, I'm here now and they're going to know about it. Who cares if they don't want me around anymore?

Me. That's who.

I walk up to Andrew and tap him on the shoulder. He spins and smiles when he sees me, letting his arm fall away from Stacie. He gives me a quick hug.

"Luce!" he yells above the band. "You made it."

Stacie gives me the once-over and says, "Hey." Then she turns to Meghan and Mateo. "I'm going to the bar. Want anything?" They both shake their heads, then Mateo comes over and gives me a kiss on the cheek. "Happy birthday, Lucy." Always the gentleman. He's a keeper.

"Thank you." I make eye contact with Meghan as he steps away. I hope I don't look too desperate.

I step toward Meghan and cup my hand over my mouth and say into her ear, "You were right about prom night. I should have talked to you guys. I didn't mean to be a drama queen. I was just confused. I'm sorry."

Meghan grabs me in a hug and yells in my ear. "Don't worry about it. You've been drama-free for so long that you were over-due. Happy birthday!"

"How was California? I've missed you."

"Cali was amazing. I've missed you too."

I look toward the bar and Connor, and Meghan's eyes follow.

She raises her eyebrows. "I knew it." Her smile is huge. "Does Liam know?"

"About Connor? He's about to find out," I respond.

My brother and Kiki watch me talking to Meghan from where they're standing, neither looking like they're going to make a move in my direction. I steel myself and walk toward them. I'm a few feet away when Drunk Shawn, a guy from our town that my brother used to jam with, accosts me.

"Sister of Liam! You are looking fine tonight." He spews whiskey breath and spit when he speaks. Gross.

Shawn graduated from high school years ago, but he still hangs around with younger kids. I half suspect he's dealing, because as far as I know, he doesn't have another job.

"Hey, Shawn." I try to keep moving but he grabs my arm. I shoot Liam a look that screams "Help!" He drops his arms from around Kiki's waist and walks toward me, looking angry and determined. When I feel a hand on my butt, I whip around, prepared to handle the creep on my own, but Connor already has a hand on Drunk Shawn's shoulder.

"Back off, man," Connor says.

Drunk Shawn throws his hands up in surrender. "Sorry, man. I didn't know she was your girl."

It looks like the whole incident is going to end peacefully enough, but then my brother gets all up in Connor's face.

"I got this," Liam says.

"Are you sure? It didn't look like it from where I was standing."

"He's my friend," Liam says.

"Your friend? You let scum like this touch your sister?" Connor is incredulous, but I get where Liam is coming from. Connor has bested him again. Saved his little sister before he had the chance. Not that Liam will ever admit that.

"Better him than you," Liam says.

"Enough!" I step between them. "Liam's right, Connor. He's got this. It's not a big deal. Right, Drun—Shawn?"

Shawn isn't so far gone that he misses his cue. "Right," he says. "See ya around, Liam. Sister of Liam."

I'm still standing between Liam and Connor when Kiki arrives. Her bangs are fuchsia. They match her face.

"Way to ruin your brother's birthday," Kiki says.

"Keeks," Liam says.

"It's Lucy's birthday too," Connor points out.

"Don't talk to my girlfriend," Liam snaps.

Seriously? What are we, ten?

"Your girlfriend *used* to be my friend." I look straight at Keeks, then I turn to my brother. "Thanks, by the way, for hijacking my life."

"You can be such a bitch sometimes. Do you know that?" Liam shouts.

Connor steps around me then and gets right in my brother's face. Liam pushes him and Connor raises his fist. Andrew tries to get between them, but not before Connor punches Liam right in the mouth. He stumbles backward and then regains his balance. I notice he's bleeding as a bouncer arrives to escort Connor to the door. I look from my brother to my boyfriend, torn.

"Liam, here let me help you." I didn't expect this night to be easy, but I didn't think it would be this bad.

Keeks puts her arm around Liam's waist. I expect her to start yelling at me, but she's pressing ice from her drink on Liam's cut and never looks at me. They start to walk away, but Liam turns and the expression on his face makes me wish I had thrown my driver's test. "I didn't hijack your life, Lucy. Maybe I just wanted to be part of it."

All the fight goes out of me. I could cry.

"Come on," Meghan says, taking my arm. "Come by us."

Andrew's eyes follow Liam, but he looks confused about what to do next. I make it easy for him. "Take care of him," I say. "I'm going to find Connor. I'll call you later."

"Okay."

I grab Andrew's hand and squeeze it. "Thanks again for the ticket. It meant a lot to me."

I'm numb as I make my way alone toward the exit. Outside in the parking lot, I find Connor leaning against his car. He opens his mouth, but I put my hand up to stop him. Nothing he can say will calm the volatile combination of hurt, anger, and sadness brewing inside me. Having him here with me was supposed to make things better, not leave me teetering on the edge of some ugly, emotional abyss. He hit my brother. *How dare he?*

"Just take me home," I say. I slam the car door so hard I'm surprised it doesn't shatter.

I don't say a word the entire car ride home. Connor apolo-
gizes over and over, but I honestly don't know what to say. He
made Liam bleed. Even if I can forgive him—and I'm not sure
I can—how can we move past that? After a while he gives up
and just glances at me from time to time with a combination
of fear and concern. It's always seemed like Connor and I never
have enough time together. Tonight, it's too much. Finally we
pull into his driveway and I say, "I thought I could bring everyone together tonight. I only made it worse."

Connor shakes his head. "No. *I* made it worse." He voice
cracks. "I shouldn't have hit your brother. I'll never forgive
myself. But when he spoke to you like that...I lost it. I'll do
whatever it takes to make it right. I'll come over tomorrow and
apologize to Liam and your parents."

My parents? Oh, God. My parents. What will they think? How
can I date the guy who hit my brother?

"Luce? Say something. How can I make this right?"

My heart is breaking—for my brother, for my friends, and
for Connor and the big mistake *he* just made that probably
cost us everything. Tears spill from my eyes, and I don't bother
to stop them.

"I wish I had been honest from the start. I wish I had told
my friends that you and I had gotten together, and—" A sob
catches in my throat.

"And what?"

I'm crying harder now, making it harder to form the words. "And I was falling in love."

"Was?" he practically whispers. "What about now?"

Connor reaches for me and stops. The tenderness and confusion on his face are too much, and I have to look way.

"I'm really tired, Connor. Can we talk about this in the morning?"

"Yeah, sure. Of course." He takes my hand but I pull it away, not knowing who I'm trying to hurt. I open the car door to get out, and the sudden brightness of the overhead light makes me squint. "Luce? Is there a chance you'll forgive me? I want to make this right."

"I know. I'm just confused right now."

"About us?"

"About us. About me and Liam. Me and my friends. I just want to be alone. To think." *To cry*.

Connor nods. "I understand. Call me when you're awake."

"I will."

"Promise?"

I nod because he sounds so desperate, but honestly, I have no idea what I'm going to do.

Chapter 28

"for some fish to survive, sometimes a change is in order. Black sea bass are hermaphrodites reproducing as both males and females at some point in their life."

From "What's Love Got to Do with It? The Dating and Mating Habits of North American Sea Life." A junior thesis by Lucy Giordano.

An angry clap of thunder wakes me from a dead sleep. I sit up and check my phone. I have five voice mails and three text messages. One from Andrew, one from Meghan, and one from Connor. Please call me, Connor's says. I'm about to listen to my voice mail when I glimpse the time. Holy crap! It's ten in the morning? I never, ever sleep this late. Ohmygod! What day is this? Where am I supposed to be?

I drop my phone and am halfway to my closet before I realize it's Saturday. I have absolutely nowhere to be and no idea where I stand with everyone in my life. Another clap of thunder rattles the panes of glass. I move to my window to close it before the rain starts. That's when I hear angry voices in the yard below.

"I came here to talk to you, not her," Connor says.

"So talk," Liam says.

Then their voices get low and it's difficult for me to pick out exact words. I don't think I want to anyway. I was up half the night, trying to think of how to fix the unfixable. I gave my heart away the day before the hurricane, and all these months later, after holding on to the idea of this boy who I believed could be everything, I've got nothing. No boyfriend, no friends, and saddest of all, no brother. *Let them argue*, I think as I slam the window. I'm so tired of it. Let them fight it out because I can't. All the fight has gone out of me. I'm done. All I want now is to get away from here.

I get dressed in a flash, then search for my Converse. When I lift the bed skirt, I see a box wrapped in blue paper. Liam's present. I totally forgot. I found *Back in Black* on vinyl on eBay. I also bought him a square frame made for album covers and some extra guitar picks. I find them all over the house—in the bowl in the kitchen where my parents keep the car keys, in the clothes basket, under the couch. I figured they'd come in handy. I bought his present a while ago, because even though he can be a total asshole sometimes, I love my brother. We share a birthday and I have always wanted to celebrate that. Sad that my gift has turned into a peace offering.

I rush down the spiral staircase, leave the present on Liam's bed, and then jog downstairs to the kitchen to grab Mom's car keys. I'm totally in for it when she finds out I took the car without asking, but I don't care. Through the screened-porch windows, I see Connor running his fingers through his hair.

He looks exasperated. Liam responds with an "F-you" and gets in Connor's face. I was going to stay out of it, but I can't let anyone get hurt again. I storm outside, keys in hand, and get between them.

"Stop it! I'm so fucking sick of this. You two don't like each other. I get it. We all get it. It's time to just accept that and move on. That's what I'm doing. Moving on."

The two of them stare at me, mouths agape, and before either can react, I sprint from the yard to Mom's car. I jump in faster than Batman, buckle up, and screech away.

My adrenaline is pumping so hard that I'm out of Seaside Park and about to drive over the bridge before it hits me: *I have no idea where I'm going*. Gram's? I'll be there soon enough. Anyway it's Saturday. She does Zumba at the senior center on Saturdays. Retired people have all the time in the world to do whatever they want, and yet they seem addicted to routine.

It starts to rain as I cross the bridge. I fumble for the wipers, then clutch the wheel at ten and two. The dark skies and wind remind me of the hurricane, and the hurricane reminds me of Connor. The rest of summer is going to feel like the aftermath of Superstorm Sandy all over again—exiled in Leisure Village and left to deal with yet another round of heartbreak and frustration caused by Connor Malloy. Only worse. This time I'm down a brother and at least one friend.

By the time I reach the traffic light on the other side of the bridge, it's pouring. Raindrops hit the windshield so hard and fast that it's like driving through a car wash. I twist the wiper controls but can't get the blades to swish faster. To make matters worse, the windows are fogging up. *Where are the defrosters?* The light turns green before I find them, and someone honks their horn at me. I roll forward but can barely see as I move into the intersection. I lean closer to the steering wheel and squint down at the road.

I'm about to put my blinker on and pull over when there's a loud screech followed by the crunch of metal as something plows into the side of the car. My head snaps against the door window, and the air bag deploys and throws me backward, hard, against the seat. I'm spinning...my head, the car, everything... Finally I jam my foot on the brake and the car skids to a stop. I have no idea what the hell just happened, and there's a loud ringing in my ears.

I don't remember hearing sirens, but at some point a police car and ambulance arrive. One minute I'm in the car, the next I'm sitting upright in the back of the ambulance. The rain has stopped, and the back doors are both open. I can see Mom's car from where I sit. Panic rises in my chest and I get dizzy. *Oh no, oh no, oh no.* The back door, on the passenger side, and part of the trunk have been pushed into the backseat.

My eyes dart around. There's a minivan in the intersection and a guy standing beside it talking to a police officer. This is not good. I close my eyes, hoping when I open them, this will all go away. My head throbs and my body aches like I have a fever.

A woman dressed all in blue, like an astronaut, is saying

something to me but I can't hear her over the ringing in my ears. I gather she's an EMT.

"What?" Am I yelling? I can't tell.

"What's your name?" This time I hear her.

"Lucy. Lucia Giordano."

"Hi, Lucy. I'm Leigh. Can you tell me how old you are?" Everything's so muffled, like I'm underwater.

"Seventeen."

"Don't worry, Lucy. You're going to be fine. They'll get you checked out at the hospital," says a male voice. Where'd he come from? Did he say something about the hospital?

"No hospital. I'll be okay as soon as this ringing stops." I have no idea how loudly or softly I'm speaking.

"Can you give us the name and number of someone to call?" Leigh says. Her hair is pulled back in a ponytail and she's wearing funky glasses. She reminds me of Meghan, so young to being doing such an important job.

I give her the first name and number I think of. "How about we chat some more?" Leigh says. "When's your birthday?"

"It was yesterday." God. *Was it only yesterday?* My seventeenth year is off to an inauspicious start.

The male EMT looks in on us again. "We're going to get moving. Buckle her up." Leigh straps me in as he slams the doors shut, and then next thing I know, I'm being whisked away in an ambulance.

At the hospital, they wheel me into an ER exam room with other people and pull a curtain around me. A doctor in scrubs

introduces herself to me as she hooks me up to a heart moni-
tor and begins an exam. She talks to me while looking in my
eyes and taking my blood pressure, but I have no idea what
I'm saying.

I'm dizzy and queasy and kind of out of it.

"Are you okay? Do you need a bedpan?" she asks.

Do I? I shake my head. "I'm good. Thanks."

But I am so not good. I've just been in a car accident, and
now I'm in the emergency room. None of this feels real. I'm
about to lose it when I hear a commotion outside the ER exam
room that grows louder right before the double doors swing
open and in walks my brother.

"Lucy!" he yells.

He looks scared and confused, but just having him here is
a relief.

"Who are you?" asks the doctor.

"Her brother." The fear and tenderness in his eyes surprise me.

The doctor nods. "Fine. Stay with her. I'll be right back. I
need to see about getting her a chest X-ray and an MRI."

"Luce. What happened?" Liam asks when the doctor's gone.

Oh no. Mom's car. The car that was supposed to get us to
work. The car we fought over. Please, let him not be mad at me.
"Liam, I'm so, so sorry. I didn't mean to wreck the car. Please
don't hate me, Liam. Please? I'm sorry."

"Hate you?" Liam takes my hand and smoothes my hair.
There's dried blood caked on his lip where it's healing. "Luce,

forget about the car. I'm just glad you're okay. When the hospital called—" His voice cracks before he continues. "I love you. You're my little sister."

Usually I'd point out that he's only three minutes older, but I hold the snark, close my eyes, and squeeze his hand. He must have thought I was going to die. "I love you too. I'm sorry Connor hit you."

He reaches up and touches his lip. "Yeah, well. I probably had that coming."

"Listen, we're going to need you to fill out some paperwork," the doctor says when she returns.

"Of course," Liam says. "Our parents are also on the way. Luce, I'll be right back, okay?"

"Promise?" It hurts to open my eyes. The lights are so bright in here.

"Promise."

I must be delirious because right before my brother leaves, I could swear he bends down and kisses my cheek.

Chapter 29

"A female pipefish will fight for her man, and once their complicated courtship begins, males and females must synchronize their speed and movements in order for a union to occur. Pipefish, like stars, must align."

From "What's Love Got to Do with It? The Dating and Mating Habits of North American Sea Life." A junior thesis by Lucy Giordano.

Around two thirty that afternoon, the four of us—me, Liam, Mom, and Dad—leave the hospital in Dad's Jeep. I don't remember the last time my family rode in one car together, and it's sad to think this is the reason. Physically, I'm not that bad. I have a mild concussion. Inside, I'm a mess. A mess *and* a terrible daughter and sister. My parents certainly didn't need this on top of everything else that's going on.

"I'm so, so sorry," I say over and over again. "I shouldn't have taken the car without asking. I ruined everything."

"You're right. You shouldn't have taken the car without asking, but you haven't ruined everything. The only thing that matters to us is that you're okay, honey," Mom says. "The car is only a hunk of metal."

"Metal that costs money," I say.

"Don't give that a second thought," Dad says. "Thank God the car bore the brunt of it."

"I can't believe that a-hole walked away without a scratch," Liam says. "He ran the red light. He could've—"

He trails off. I get it. I'm glad he didn't finish that sentence. I smile at my brother and hope my gratitude shows.

"Hey, I forgot to ask. How did you get to the hospital, Liam?" Even if he wanted to drive without a license, I had the only available vehicle.

Liam reaches into his pocket and pulls out the necklace from Connor. My heart constricts as I take it from him and fold it into my hand. It must have come off in Connor's car last night. I look out my window and don't say anything. I can't. Dad turns on the radio, the sports station, which prompts a discussion between him and Mom about the All-Star game.

"He wanted to wait and see you," Liam says in a low voice. "But the X-rays took a while and his dad needed him for something in North Jersey."

My eyes flash toward our parents. Liam understands. "I didn't tell them what happened. I *won't* tell them what happened."

"Thank you."

"He apologized. And so did I. He also told me all about the volunteer work he's doing."

I raise my eyebrows in a question. *Ouch!* This has got to be the worst headache I've ever had, but the doctors won't let me take anything stronger than Tylenol or Advil. They don't want the potential side effects of prescription pain meds, like dizziness or disorientation, to be confused with symptoms of more significant head trauma.

"We had a lot of time to talk," Liam answers.

Liam and Connor were sitting in the waiting room together, talking? "I'm trying to picture that."

Mom switches the station and Dad starts complaining about how he doesn't want to listen to NPR.

"Yeah. I'm going to join him on the next rebuild project."

"*Really?*" I don't mean to sound so incredulous, but last night the two of them wanted to beat each other senseless.

"What? I'm good with a hammer."

"But are you good with a hammer and other sharp tools around Connor?" Saying his name out loud makes my chest hurt as much as my head.

"We're cool."

"You're *cool?*" I'm dubious. "You're so not cool."

"Okay. Maybe we're not quite there yet. Give it time. Anyway, he asked me to join his *Restore the Shore* team on the next job and it was hard to say no."

"Why?"

"Because it's close by. In Seaside."

"Oh. Well, great. That sounds great."

It is great, right? I touch my fingers to my temple and hope this isn't another delusional moment brought on by the concussion.

• • ● • •

We get home around midafternoon, and Andrew is waiting on the front steps. Correction: Andrew and a fish are waiting on the front steps. I squint to be sure. Yup. It's a fish. In a bowl.

"I texted him from the hospital," Liam says.

"Uh...thanks?"

Dad helps me out of the car as Andrew approaches with the fish. "Your mom and I dropped everything and left in a rush. We need to go back to work for a few hours, sweetie. The boys will keep an eye on you. Right?"

"Of course," Andrew says. He hands me the small glass bowl with rainbow-colored stones on the bottom and an aqua-colored betta swimming around. "I didn't think you'd want flowers."

"I love him," I say. I can tell by the coloring and shape of its fins that it's a male. I talk to the fish. "Hi, Kermit."

"Kermit's a frog," Liam says.

"This one's a fish."

"It must be the concussion," Andrew says.

We all walk into the house where Mom insists I stay downstairs so Liam and Andrew can keep an eye on me. The doctor said I can sleep if I want to, but advised that someone should check on me every few hours to make sure I'm responsive. I guess we'll sit around and watch the flat-screen TV. At least we have a few weeks to enjoy it before the renters move in.

"I brought movies," Andrew says. He waves the Lord of the Rings trilogy and every *Star Wars* episode in my face.

"Aren't you supposed to keep me *awake*?" I joke.

"I've got the first three seasons of *The Walking Dead*," Liam offers.

"You're gonna watch with us?" The thought makes my heavy head lighter. It's been too long since I've hung out with my brother.

Liam shrugs. "I don't have to be at work until later."

I smile. "Plenty of time for the zombie apocalypse."

• • ● • •

Liam and Andrew make good babysitters. They let me doze off after the fourth episode, then wake me to give me fluids and check my pupils for dilation. Andrew looked up "concussions" on WebMD and now he thinks he's an expert.

When my parents get home around seven, Mom invites Andrew to stay for dinner. We get pizza and ziti from our favorite place, but I'm not all that hungry. After we eat, my parents take a walk, and Liam goes to work. I'm assuming Keeks drove him, and I try not to feel bad about her not stopping in. Andrew and I sit at the kitchen table playing chess. It must be the minor head trauma because he's kicking my butt, which hardly ever happens, and I can't seem to muster the energy to care.

I cover my mouth and yawn. "*The Lord of the Rings* is sounding pretty good right now."

Andrew checks his phone. "As much as I'd like Liv Tyler to talk Elfish to me, I want to swing by my house before work."

I shoo him away. "Go. Go. I'll put the board away." It's been nice having him around. Almost like old times, before we kissed and screwed up our friendship.

"I don't want to leave you alone."

"My parents will be back soon."

They usually do a six-mile loop on the boardwalk. But something tells me that's not going to be long enough to de-stress after the wrench I've thrown into our already precarious financial situation. Thanks to me, we're down one car, at least temporarily. That's in addition to our storm-ravaged rental bungalow that needs to be redone. Forget the Marine Mammal Stranding Center. I have no way to get there now. It's all so overwhelming that I don't mean to, but I start to cry.

"Luce. Everything's going to be all right." Andrew pushes his chair away from the table and quickly grabs some paper towels from the roll on the counter. Then he bends down beside my chair and hands me a huge wad of Bounty. The sight of all that absorbent paper makes me giggle through my tears.

"What am I supposed to do with that?" I ask.

"Uh, blow your nose?"

"There's enough here to clean the kitchen floor."

"Wipe Smaug's ass?"

Now I can't stop laughing.

"See? They really are the quicker picker-upper," he says and then opens his arms for a hug.

It feels good to wrap my arms around him. Not spine-tingling, heart-pounding good, just normal good. And normal good is good.

"I missed you," I say.

"I'm here," he says.

"What about everyone else?" I say.

"Why don't you ask them yourself? I texted Kiki and Meghan. They're both coming by later."

It'll be good to see Meghan. At the club last night, I felt like we were almost back to good. But Kiki? Maybe she'll decide not to come. Andrew reads my mind.

"Don't worry. Keeks is cool. She didn't like the way Liam screamed at you either."

My head feels like the Road Runner dropped an anvil on it, but hearing that Keeks and I have a chance makes me feel better.

Andrew stands to leave. "Are you sure you're going to be okay?"

"Yeah, I think I'm going to go up to my room for a while."

"Oh no, you're not. No stairs until your head is better. Your parents gave me strict orders."

"Fine." I guess I'll be sleeping down here tonight.

Before Andrew leaves the kitchen, he looks down at me and says, "Call him. Let him know you're okay."

"Who?"

"Luce." Andrew sighs and walks back toward me.

"He hit Liam," I say.

"Because of what Liam said about you. Connor loves you. He did what any guy who loves you would have done."

"How do you know?" I know how he knows. I see it in his eyes.

"Because I felt like hitting Liam myself."

"Andrew..."

He holds up his hand.

I nod my head and smile. "I love you too."

"I know." Then Andrew leaves for work.

As expected, my parents don't want me sleeping in my room. They're afraid I'll need the bathroom in the middle of the night and pass out as I walk down the stairs or something. Mom sets up the couch with my pillow, comforter, and Frenchie right before she and Dad go up for the night. Kiki and Meghan arrive about ten minutes later, interrupting my mental Ping-Pong game as I weigh the pros and cons of calling Connor.

The first few minutes brim with weirdness. Keeks and I can't make eye contact, but I manage to avoid awkward silences by offering them a way-too-descriptive account of my accident and trip to the ER.

Though she loves a good medical drama more than most, Meghan finally tackles the elephant in the room. "What happened with you and Connor?" That's all it takes for me to tell them everything. Not "Ew, too-much-information everything" but everything. Maybe my head injury affected that part of my brain prone to keeping secrets, but it's such a relief to no longer have that all balled up inside me.

"I wish you had said something to us sooner," Kiki says.

Me too.

"I'm not surprised," Meghan says. "There's always been something between you and Connor."

She's right. But for some reason I always thought I needed to hide my secret crush on the summer boy next door. In retrospect, I guess I didn't fool anyone. "How could you tell?"

Kiki chimes in: "The way you watched each other. I knew when Connor walked onto the beach. It was like your whole demeanor changed if he was around. It went both ways. Like there was an invisible pull between you. Even when he was with another girl, he always searched you out."

An invisible pull. *Like gravity*, I think, *but harder to pin down with a numerical value.* "So no professional poker in my future?"

"I don't know about cards, but Connor definitely is," Meghan says.

"I'm not so sure."

"I am." Kiki gives my hand a squeeze. She sounds so sure that it gives me hope.

After Meghan and Kiki leave, I sit on the screened-in porch and dial Connor's number. It goes straight to voice mail. I'm about to hang up but decide to leave a message at the last second. I talk too fast, afraid I might get cut off.

"Hey. It's me. I just wanted to say thanks for driving my brother to the hospital. I'm sorry about last night. I was confused. I should have given you a chance to make things right. I do forgive you. And about that thing I said…the falling-in-love thing? I'm sorry if I made it sound like it was in the past—" I get cut off before I can finish. I don't get to tell him I never stopped falling.

I spend the rest of the night waiting for a call, a text, anything. And just when I decide that I can't begin another cycle of waiting for Connor, my phone rings. I'm watching a story about typhoons on the Weather Channel because I've given up on everything else.

"How are you?" Connor asks.

"My heads hurts."

Connor sighs. "Luce, I want you to know I'm so sorry."

I assume he means about Liam. "It's okay. Liam is moving past it. I'm sorry for being so hard on you."

"Luce, this isn't just about Liam. It's about me screwing up your life. I feel like all of this is my fault. If I hadn't come over this morning and argued with your brother. If I hadn't hit him last night… I keep making life harder for you, Luce, and that's the last thing I want to do. God, if anything worse had happened to you—"

"Connor, stop. It's not your fault. Some guy ran a red light. It was an accident."

"But you were driving in the pouring rain because of me."

There's a long silence. Neither of us knows what to say.

"Listen," Connor says. "My dad has a job he needs help with. I think I'm going to stay up here for a while."

"Connor, please…?" Tears form behind my eyes and betray something in my voice.

"Luce, see? All I do is make your life harder."

"It's not you. It's been a long day. I haven't slept…"

"You should get some rest. I'm going to hang up now. I…I'll see you soon. Promise."

He disconnects before I can respond. The tears are falling too fast now for me to form words anyway.

I sit up to put my phone on the coffee table and see Liam is standing there. For how long, I have no idea. Then I hear Mom's footsteps on the stairs coming down to make her umpteenth check on me. Liam stops her before she reaches the landing.

"Mom, go back to bed. I've got this. I'll stay down here tonight and keep an eye on Lucy."

"Are you sure, hon? That would be great."

"Yeah. I'm sure."

Mom calls around the corner. "Good night, sweetie. Liam's going to take care of you."

That's something I don't hear every day.

"Night, Mom," I manage to squeak out.

Liam walks over to the coffee table, grabs the tissues, and hands them to me. "I'll be right back. Gonna run upstairs to grab a blanket and pillow."

I nod. I must look pathetic. "Thank you."

He walks toward the steps, then reverses course.

"Luce?"

"Yeah?"

"I've been a crappy brother."

"Liam, it's okay. I haven't been the greatest sister."

Liam gives an ironic laugh. "I think the only thing I'm better at than you is being a shitty sibling. I should be looking out for you."

"I can take care of myself."

"I know you can." He sits down on the edge of the couch. "I thought I was doing what was best for you. I didn't think he was good enough. At least that's what I told myself. But I was also selfish. I was pissed at Connor for being with Nat. I wanted to punish him by not letting him be with you."

"Natalie's the one who hurt you, not Connor."

"I can see that now, but at the time—"

"You still loved Natalie."

Liam nods. He looks so dejected that I can tell he's being sincere. "It's okay, Liam. I get it. I might have done the same thing."

Liam scoffs. "Are you kidding me? No, you wouldn't have. You're the good twin. The smart twin. The one who gets her brother the perfect birthday present, even when he doesn't deserve it. I'm the screwup."

I'd forgotten all about leaving the AC/DC album in his room. "We've both done our sharing of screwing up, Liam. Screwing up is normal. It's human. It's what we do after, to make things right, that matters."

"I know. And I'm going to make it up to you. I owe you a birthday gift, and I'm working on something perfect. It's just going to take a little while before it comes together. But you're going to love it. Just wait."

His enthusiasm makes me totally curious. Maybe it's a new saltwater fish tank? That would be awesome. "You don't have to make anything up to me, Liam. I don't need presents. I just want us to be close again. Like when we were little."

"You were my first friend."

"It's about time we became best friends."

"Agreed." Liam slaps his hands against his thighs and moves to stand. "Well, I'm gonna get my stuff."

Liam's head is probably about to explode with the deluge of openness that's been happening around here. I know the feeling. Still, I push it a little further. What the hell, right? I grab hold of his arm.

"Writing, surfing, Spanish, Ping-Pong, Scrabble, sleeping, dating, mini-golf, world history, *guitar*, and just about every video game ever invented…"

Liam's confused.

"A few of the things you're better at. And let's not forget songwriting. Your songs? They're amazing."

"Yeah?"

I nod. "Yeah. Definitely."

Liam smiles so big before he heads upstairs that it makes me regret not saying something sooner. I hope he's not too tired when he gets back with the blanket and pillow. We've got a lot of catching up to do.

Chapter 30

"Stone throwing, melodic singing, elaborate aerials—mating season for the piping plover is a tumultuous affair. The small seabirds are mostly monogamous and the male goes to great lengths to find a missus for life, including impressing her with his nest-building skills."

From "What's Love Got to Do with It? The Dating and Mating Habits of North American Sea Life." A junior thesis by Lucy Giordano.

It's recovery day six for me. I'm the one who got concussed, but since my accident, we've all done a lot of healing. My head stopped hurting, and Liam no longer looks like he's been punched in the mouth. Mom's getting a brand-new car with money from the insurance company, and I'll begin working at the Marine Mammal Stranding Center next week. The internship supervisor was totally sympathetic about my accident and agreed to let me start later.

Yesterday Chad sent me a picture of himself and his new fiancée, and tonight I'm having rocky road ice cream (it seemed apropos) with Kiki at the Sundae Times. My tiny corner of the universe would be copacetic if we weren't moving to Gram's in three weeks and I'd seen or spoken to Connor.

"I'm taking a ride to the stranding center on Sunday," I tell Kiki as we sit down at a table outside. "I want to find out exactly where it is and how long it will take me to get there."

"Enough with the sick sea mammals." Kiki brushes back her bangs, which are the exact color of her black raspberry yogurt. I swear she picked that flavor on purpose. "Have you heard from Connor?"

My mood sinks. "He texted me. Once."

"What'd he say?"

"'Has anyone ordered the Tsunami?'"

"That's it?"

"He's trying to keep things light, I guess."

"Sounds like he's trying to keep things corny." Her hand shoots up to her mouth and her eyes bug out.

I try to smile. "It's okay. I know."

"He'll be back soon. I'll bet anything."

When Connor and I spoke after my accident, I thought he was just upset when he said he wanted to keep his distance for a while. I was sure he would change his mind and be back the next day. But it's been a week. I wake up every morning thinking I've heard his truck in the driveway between our houses, but when I look out my bedroom window, he isn't there.

"I wouldn't bet on seeing him anytime soon," I say. "If and when he does come back, I might already be at Gram's."

Kiki looks concerned. "I'm sorry. I shouldn't have brought him up. You need a break from thinking about Connor. We should spend the whole day on the beach tomorrow."

"Aren't we working the same shift at Breakwater Burrito?"

Kiki slumps. "Oh yeah. Sunday?"

"Stranding center? Remember?"

Kiki doinks herself in the head. "Duh, that's right. You said that." Her face brightens. "I can go with you! We can stop in Ocean City afterward. I love the boardwalk there. I mean... only if you want me to come."

"Yeah, of course. Why wouldn't I?"

"Maybe because I've been a shitty friend."

"Me too. I should have told you about Connor from the start. You always tell me everything. Not telling isn't a lie, but it is a betrayal. I get that now."

She shrugs. "We both made mistakes. But there's still plenty of summer left. Hey, you should sleep over tomorrow. Better yet, stay with me and Mom in August. I'll ask her, but I know she'll totally say yes. She loves you. We can be together every day like we used to be."

Keeks's generous offer sounds wonderful. A chance to revisit old times. It's been awhile since we've done a sleepover. But staying with Keeks and her mom in a two-room apartment for a month is a whole different thing.

I rest my hand on Kiki's. "Thanks so much for the offer, Keeks. Maybe I can spend a few Friday or Saturday nights with you? Gram will be disappointed if I don't stay with her. She's kinda looking forward to me being there. She likes to tell me everything that's happened on her soap opera. In great detail."

"That's cute that she likes to share her stories with you," Keeks says.

It is. But fictional drama's got nothing on the stories I have for Gram. They'll make her want to turn off the TV.

· • ◉ • ·

That night I toss and turn for who knows how long before I give up and turn on the light. It's too quiet. I can hear myself think, and that's the last thing I want to do. I reach for my music. There's a tap on my door before I can get my earbuds in.

"Luce?"

It's Liam. He's checked on me every night since the accident, even though I've been perfectly fine for days.

"Come in."

The door opens a crack and he looks in. "Hey, did I wake you?"

"Nah, I can't sleep."

"Me neither," he says.

"That's nothing new for you."

"True." Liam steps all the way into my room. "Kiki says that she asked her mom and it's totally fine for you to stay with them in August. She wanted you to know."

I have to admit that I didn't expect the two of them to last this long, but if they make each other happy, I'm happy. It's nice to have my brother included in my group of friends, which much like the rest of the island, is in a rebuilding phase. Or maybe it's more like it's undergoing a remodel with an addition. Andrew's been spending more time with Stacie, so it looks like she may be joining the inner sanctum soon. To be honest, I'm not sure how I feel about that, but I'll deal. It's not about me; it's about Andrew.

"That's really nice of her," I tell Liam. "She mentioned it this afternoon. I'll see how it goes at Gram's first. Maybe I'll take Kiki up on the offer later in the summer. I wouldn't want to push things between us or overstay my welcome."

"I feel the same way about staying with Andrew. I'll probably just be there until…" Liam trails off.

"Until when?"

"Until he gets sick of me."

"So I'll see you at Gram's in August?" I laugh, and Liam grabs a teddy bear off my dresser and throws it at me.

"Very funny, Luce. If the marine biology thing doesn't work out, you should consider stand-up."

"I might just do that." I'm glad we can kid each other again without the venom.

"Well, anyway. I just wanted to tell you about Kiki."

"Thanks for the update."

Liam puts his hand on the door. "Luce?"

"Yeah?"

"Don't worry. Everything's going to be fine. You'll see."

I want to believe him, and I know on some level he's right. The rental money will help us rebuild the cottage, so hopefully next year at this time, this will all seem like a distant, bad memory. Maybe by then, my chest won't tighten and my insides won't feel so hollow when I think about Connor.

After Liam leaves, I turn off the AC and open both windows as wide as they go. I want to hear the ocean while I still can, letting the waves lull me to sleep before thoughts of the Big Mistake creep into my head and convince me that I've made even more of a mess.

· • ● • ·

The next morning I wake up to the sound of hammering. *The Valentinos are finally fixing their shed*, I think as I roll over. I've been sleeping later since the accident, and after a restless night, I was hoping to stay in bed until at least seven thirty. But the hammering gets louder. Actually, it sounds more like a sledgehammer—or wrecking ball—splintering wood. Frustrated, I reach for my earbuds. Then comes the *beep, beep, beep* of a construction vehicle in reverse. *Holy crap, it's loud!* It's as if the noise is right outside. I kick off the covers and head to my bedroom window—the one facing the backyard.

I pull up the shade, and it takes my brain a full thirty seconds to catch up with what my eyes are seeing. Guys in green shirts are prying out the windows of our falling-down rental cottage, throwing boards and glass into a Dumpster sitting in our driveway. Dad is outside, a coffee mug in his hand, talking to Connor's father. My eyes pan to the cottage's roof and...is that...*Liam and Connor*...ripping up shingles?

"Hey!" I yell as loud as I can.

No one hears me above the racket. I wait for a lull in the beeping and hammering, then yell again. This time Dad sees me at the window and raises his hand. He points to the cottage as if to say, "See?" Then he puts his fingers in his mouth and whistles at Liam and Connor. They both turn and look toward my window. Connor cups his hands around his mouth and screams, "Lucy Goosey! What up?" In my haste to wave back, I smack my head on the window frame.

"Careful!" Liam yells. "No one has time to take you to the hospital today!"

The image of Connor and Liam together on that roof is unbelievable. They might as well be Santa and the Easter Bunny. I duck back inside, then pull on my Breakwater Burrito tee and jean shorts before running downstairs barefoot. Mom is on the screened-in porch and watching through the windows. She opens her arms wide and hugs me.

"How?" I mumble into her shoulder.

"Connor and his father made it happen. Liam too," Mom says. She doesn't offer details, but there's time for that later. I move to go outside, but she points to my feet.

"Shoes! There are all kinds of nails and debris out there."

I slip on Mom's flips that are by the door. "The renters?"

"The heavy construction will be done by August. We told them what was happening and they don't seem to mind renting this house, like they originally planned, while the cottage is being finished."

"Why didn't you tell me?"

"Liam wanted it to be a surprise. A belated birthday present."

By the time I get outside, Liam has come down from the roof and is standing by Dad. I throw my arms around him. While I hug him, my eyes dart between the guys in green shirts and hard hats. I don't see Connor. "You're right. This is the perfect gift. I can't believe you didn't tell me."

Liam steps back and smiles at me. "I almost did. Last night. I *did* say our project was in Seaside."

"Tell her the best part," Dad says, putting his arm around me and giving me a squeeze.

"Connor's dad is donating a crew, which means the job will move faster, and we might be able to move into the cottage before summer's over."

"I should really thank Connor and his dad," I say.

"They had to leave." Liam squeezes my arm and gives me a knowing look. "Connor said he'll see you later."

It's nice to have my brother on my side again.

Chapter 31

"You can count on two hands, maybe one, the number of species that mate for life. Love, the romantic kind, the obsessive kind, and sometimes even the unconditional kind, is counterintuitive to the propagation of the species and survival, and yet when it's right and pure, it can be the one thing above all else that makes every second of your life worth living."

Handwritten addendum to "What's Love Got to Do with It? The Dating and Mating Habits of North American Sea Life." A junior thesis by Lucy Giordano.

I walk in to Breakwater Burrito around lunchtime and see Kiki standing in the kitchen.

"The cottage is getting fixed!" I'm being super loud but I can't help it. "Like right now!"

"I know! It was sooo hard to keep my mouth shut yesterday."

She grabs my hands. Her raspberry bangs bounce in and out of her eyes as we jump up and down together celebrating like two five-year-olds. The cottage, Andrew, Kiki... Little by little, the pieces of my life that were scattered by the storm are coming back together.

"I'm happy for you, hon," Adela says to me. "Hurricane Sandy was a bitch. I'd punch her in the face if I could. But seeing friends and family get back what she took is even better."

After the initial excitement, the day drags. I'm finding the sound track tedious—usually I can listen to Weezer's "Island in the Sun" ten times a day, no problem—and the customers annoying. I'm not even in the mood for chips and guac, and I'm *always* in the mood for chips and guac. It's all me, I know. There's a nervous, excited energy building in me, and if I don't see Connor soon, I might implode. I texted him this morning but haven't heard back.

"Hey, Lucy," Michael says. He's ringing up takeout customers and I'm on the other register. "Does your brother still play guitar?"

"Yeah, why?"

"My friend's band is playing at the yacht club next weekend, but their guitarist will be away. Do you think he'd sub?"

"It depends. What kind of music do they play?"

"A little bit of everything. They're a cover band."

I take a napkin and write Liam's number on it. "He's working on our cottage right now, but tell your friend to call him."

"Hey, that's awesome. About your cottage. I heard you tell Kiki the news when you got here." He laughs. "I think the whole block heard you tell Kiki the news when you got here."

I giggle. "Uh, yeah. Sorry 'bout that. It's kind of a big deal."

Michael smiles. "It's totally a big deal. No worries. My hearing came back."

He's joking, of course, but he reminds me. Mine did too. My ears rang for two days after getting walloped by the air bag. I was beginning to think I had permanent hearing loss or tinnitus. My physical activity is still restricted due to the concussion (no surfing or skateboarding), but thankfully my ears are working fine.

Around three, Andrew pops in for a beef burrito and gives me the update. "The demolition is going well."

"Did everyone know about this except me?"

"Pretty much," Andrew says as he chews the end of his straw. "Surprise!"

He places a to-go order for the small army of contractors at my house, then eats at a table by the window while he waits. We're too busy for me to go on break, but I wish I could join him and get more specific details about the work being done.

Before Andrew leaves, he walks around the long line to pick up the to-go orders. Michael hands him a large shopping bag with the food, then Andrew slaps something on the counter and slides it in my direction. "Almost forgot. I saw Connor when I stopped by your house. He told me to give this to you."

He lifts his hand, and my stomach jumps and lands somewhere near my tonsils. The sparkly sea-horse key chain…I ignore what my customer is saying—*chicken taco, blah, blah, I know, I know*—and pick it up. My eyes find Andrew's. "Did he say anything?"

"Yep. He said, 'Tell her six o'clock. She'll know where.'"

I tuck the key in my back pocket and try to hold it together, but I am freaking out! I hate that there's a counter between Andrew and me right now. "I could kiss you, you know that?" I tell him.

"Yeah, well. I am *irresistible*. But I wouldn't want to get in Connor's way. Dude can throw a punch. Later." He gives me a two-fingered salute and then he's gone, leaving me to get through the next two hours without going insane!

Adela tells me to take my break at four thirty, but I ask to work straight through and leave early instead.

At home, everything is quiet. The workers have left but not before making tremendous progress in just one day. The sorry-looking, falling-down structure that was our cottage is gone, and in its place are the two-by-four bones of what it will become. The entire yard smells like fresh lumber, and for the first time since Hurricane Sandy, the scent doesn't bother me. I'm ready for a new life in my old town.

Inside I find Dad drinking a beer and watching the Mets game.

"I can't believe how much they got done," I say.

"We'll be back here in no time, sweets," Dad says. The storm damage has been hard on my parents. I don't remember the last time he looked so relaxed.

"Where's Liam?" I ask.

"He left for work with Andrew."

"After working outside all day? He's going to be wiped."

Dad chuckles. "It'll be good for him. I hate to think that it took a terrible accident to get him motivated, but since then, your brother has really been stepping up."

"I know," I say. I'm proud of him.

"Sit," Dad says. "Watch the game."

I glance at my phone. Five thirty! "I'd love to, Dad, but I've gotta—" I bend down and kiss his cheek. "I'm going to shower."

Ten minutes later, I'm in a bra and panties with my hair wrapped in a towel and tearing my closet apart as I look for something to wear. I discover a navy blue sundress that I love but had totally forgotten about and my tan sandals with the wedge that I haven't worn since my National Honor Society induction.

I rummage through my makeup bag and retrieve my apricot lip gloss. I give my lips two quick swipes and my eyelashes a coat of black mascara. Next I run a brush through my still-damp hair but decide to let it air-dry on the way. Then I fly as fast as my shoes will allow me down two flights of stairs and swoosh past my dad with a breathless, "I'm-meeting-a-friend-and-I'll-be-careful-see-you-bye."

"Tell Connor I said 'hello,'" my father calls after me as the screen door slams.

I briefly consider taking my bike, but that's another restricted activity, so I set off on foot toward Ocean Avenue. As I walk, I take yogalike breaths. *You shouldn't look like you've been running*, I tell myself. I take it slow for two blocks, not wanting to turn my ankle in what, for me, are high heels. By the third block I give up on my wedges altogether, kick them off, and speed walk. Four blocks later, I stop dead when the place comes into view.

I look at the widow's walk. It's empty. In the distance the bell on a child's bike rings, but other than that, all is quiet. Still. There isn't even a breeze. The heavy air smells sweet with the hydrangea surrounding the big wrap-around porch. My eyes keep searching…Connor. He's sitting on the top step. He stands when he sees me, and I start running—key in one hand, shoes in the other—until I reach the path. I hesitate for a moment. When he starts walking down the steps, I let my sandals slip from my hands and rush into his arms.

He catches me, lifts me up, and twirls me around. My lips touch his neck, and I breathe him in as he buries his face in my damp hair. When my bare feet are back on the hot stone, he holds my face in his hands and kisses me, and all our time apart dissipates as this calm summer night converges with that tumultuous October day.

When we separate, Connor smiles at me and offers his hand. I hesitate and look toward the front door. "Bob and Jane?" I ask.

"Two-week Mediterranean cruise."

"Good for them."

I place my hand in his and let the key ring dangle from my pinkie. We walk up the stairs together and onto the big wooden porch, where a café table has been set for dinner. Tea-light candles flicker between real china plates, and two wineglasses have been filled with iced tea. The sand dunes and boardwalk across the street reflect in the large picture window behind the table. It looks like a photograph, the kind you wish you could step right into.

"What's this?" I ask.

"The beginning. Where we start again."

Where have I heard that before? "That's what Madame Ava said!"

Connor wraps his arms around my waist and kisses me again. "Best fifty bucks I ever spent."

He leads me toward the table and pulls out my chair. I like the view from the porch. The widow's walk can wait. It survived the storm. It's not going anywhere.

Author's Note

Superstorm Sandy was the largest Atlantic hurricane in history. With sustained winds of seventy-five miles per hour, an eight-and-a-half-foot storm surge, and winds spanning 1,100 miles across, it originated in the Caribbean—affecting countries including Haiti, Jamaica, Cuba, and the Dominican Republic—and eventually crept up the Eastern Seaboard like a slow-moving giant.

More than two hundred eighty people died, and twenty-four U.S. states were affected. New Jersey and New York were hit particularly hard when the mega-sized hurricane slammed into their shores on October 29, 2012, causing mass destruction. In New York City, streets and subways were flooded, and U.S. stock trading was suspended for two straight days. In New Jersey, twelve people lost their lives; 2.7 million were left without power; 37,000 primary residences were destroyed or damaged; and 8.7 million cubic yards of debris were left in the storm's wake. Today, the effort to rebuild in New Jersey is ongoing, especially in those towns closest to the shore. For more information or to help visit:

sandynjrelieffund.org
state.nj.us/gorr
fema.gov/new-jersey-sandy-recovery-0
nj.com/hurricanesandy

Acknowledgments

I love the New Jersey shore. It's a beautiful and special place—home to thousands and home away from home to thousands more. I'd like to acknowledge all those who lost so much during Superstorm Sandy and thank everyone who's played a part in restoring the shore. I'm grateful for the opportunity to share Lucy's story and through her show readers this place that means so much to so many.

Many talented and generous people made this book possible and I would like to thank the following:

Kerry Sparks, who's more than an amazing agent, she's my sounding board, my cheerleader, my sometimes therapist, and dear friend.

Annette Pollert-Morgan, for believing in me—again—and always making everything I write better. I'm thrilled to be working with you a second time!

The wonderful team at Sourcebooks, Dominique Raccah, Todd Stocke, Kate Prosswimmer, Sarah Cardillo, Kelly Lawler, Nicole Komasinski, Elizabeth Boyer, Melanie Jackson, Valerie Pierce, Beth Oleniczak, Amelia Narigon, Chris Bauerle, Sean Murray, and Vanessa Han, thank you for a gorgeous cover that captures the mood of this novel perfectly.

Chris Jordan and Kathy Dzielak of the *Asbury Park Press* for giving me my rock star moment.

Martha Alderson, a.k.a. The Plot Whisperer, whose books and wisdom opened my mind during revision.

Meghan McCauley, who generously took the time to answer all my questions about growing up in Seaside Park.

Mary Jo Martone, who first told me about ReClam the Bay, and the organization's dedicated volunteers for the inspiring work they're doing to reclaim Barnegat Bay.

The Borough of Seaside Park, for being the kind of place where I love spending time, in real life and in my head.

Lori Lawson, who makes my website look pretty and always answers questions from this tech-challenged writer.

Liz Faleska, who answered my questions about emergency room procedure.

Early readers, Lainie Lederman and Stephanie Charlefour, who gave me great feedback, and encouragement.

My always reader and *comadre,* Adriana Calderon, who I never publish a word without, and Jen Post, an expert in biology, twins, the Heisenberg Uncertainty Principle, and keeping me sane. Love you both.

The talented authors at YA Outside the Lines, the Lucky 13s, and in cyberspace—meeting you all has been a great gift on this journey. At the end of *Charlotte's Web*, Wilbur says it's not very often that someone is both a true friend and a good writer. Thank you to the following people for being both: Melissa Azarian, Bethany Crandell, Lisa Reiss, Sharon Biggs Waller, and especially Jen Mann, who was with me every word of the way.

Special thanks to my ridiculously supportive family and friends (you know who you are), and all the readers, librarians, bloggers, writers, and booksellers, who have taken the time to read and support my books.

Mom and Dad, Mom D. and Dad D., Melissa, Anthony, Cassie, and Anthony James—thank you. Your love and support make everything possible and I love you all.

Mike, my best friend and partner in this crazy ride, I don't know where I'd be without you, and Carley, our brilliant and beautiful daughter, who came up with name "Lucy" and will someday write better books than her mom. You give me the love, support, and space (it's small, but I'll take it) to pursue my dreams. Three is the magic number. I love you both so much! Thank you, God, for this moment and each one that follows.

About the Author

Jennifer Salvato Doktorski is the author of two other YA novels, *How My Summer Went Up in Flames* and *Famous Last Words*. She lives with her family in New Jersey and spends her summers "down the shore," where she dreams of taking surfing lessons and observes sea life while keeping her toes in the sand.

FALL IN LOVE WITH THE HUNDRED OAKS SERIES FROM

Miranda Kenneally

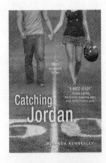
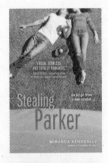

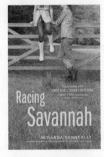
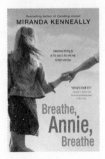
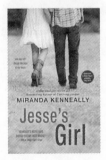

For more about Miranda Kenneally, visit:

mirandakenneally.com

THE TRUTH ABOUT US

Janet Gurtler

BESTSELLING AUTHOR OF *I'M NOT HER.*

THEY NEVER MEANT TO FALL IN LOVE.

When Jess is caught drinking, her dad orders her to spend the rest of the summer volunteering at the local soup kitchen. Thrust into a world where her own problems no longer seem so insurmountable, Jess meets Flynn, a guy from her high school who comes to the soup kitchen for meals with his adorable little brother. Slowly, Jess and Flynn begin to know and trust each other, despite the prejudice of their families. But as their relationship intensifies and outside pressures escalate, can they find the strength to stay together?

For more about Janet Gurtler, visit:

janet-gurtler.com

JULIANA STONE

USA TODAY BESTSELLING AUTHOR

"The classic miscommunication, the emotional pushing and pulling, the 'will she?' and 'won't he?' of the destined-to-be-in-love. Readers of Miranda Kenneally, Jenny Han, and Susane Colasanti will enjoy Stone."

—*VOYA* on *Boys Like You*

For more about Juliana Stone, visit:

julianastone.com

THE SUMMER OF SKINNY DIPPING

Amanda Howells

**THE LIGHT FLASHED THREE TIMES. I SIGNALED
BACK. THIS WAS HOW SIMON AND I MET UP FOR
OUR MIDNIGHT WALKS ON THE BEACH...**

After getting dumped by her boyfriend, sixteen-year-old Mia Gordon is
looking forward to spending a relaxing summer in the Hamptons with her
glamorous cousins. But when she arrives, her cousins are distant, moody,
and caught up with a fast crowd. Mia finds herself lonelier than ever.

That's when she meets her next-door neighbor, Simon Ross. Simon
isn't like the snobby party boys her cousins seem obsessed with; he's funny,
artistic, and utterly adventurous. And from the very first time he encourages
Mia to go skinny-dipping, she's caught up in a current impossible to resist.